THE CODE OF LIFE

Luke Moore

Printed in the United States of America
ISBN: 0985496509
The Code of Life-ISBN-978-0-9854965-0-0
"Library of Congress Control Number: 2013902317
Norman L Moore, Logan, Ohio

This book is a work of fiction. The sequences of events regarding the Lewis and Clark expedition are not guaranteed to be accurate.

Luke Moore

*This book is dedicated
to my wife Debra.
Without her help
this book wouldn't exist.*

Thank You Barb,
Pam, Sherry,
Tina, Jill.
Your friendship,
my treasure.

PROLOG

A daytime storm raged with never before seen ferocity. An hour earlier the sun burned brightly. But then cold dark clouds swept in on hurricane class winds, turning the day into night. Rare storms such as this one sent some people of the prehistoric age to commune with their deities, asking forgiveness. Some made sacrifices to try and pacify the angry Gods.

Others watched the storm in wonder of nature in conflict with itself. Taking notice of atmospheric changes that caused deviations such as the one they were being witness to.

Lightning streaked across the dark low hanging clouds creating a strobe like view of the surrounding landscape. Trees whipped and waved frantically in the wind. The ground trembled with each mighty rumble of thunder.

Yet, standing majestically, as it had for millions of years; is a rugged, rocky face of a bluff. It reigns over the land, silent but strong. Much like a sentry, the stone face of the bluff looks towards the west, out over the land. A narrow river, flows along the base.

Midway between the bottom of the bluff and its flattened plateau is a jagged hole. A flickering amber light illuminates that opening. There is a makeshift ladder, barely perceptible within the jumble of fallen stone and cascading rain water at the bluffs base. This crud ladder leads to the hole.

Though thunder shakes the land, booming of a different sort bellows from within the dimly lit hole in the rocky wall.

Hidden within the hole, is a cavern. In this cavern a huge fire burns brightly, the source of the amber glow. Flaming embers fly high then vanish into the overhead blackness. The disturbing smoke and noise cause cave dwelling bats to stir, dive, and then settle again, unseen in the blackness.

Contorted shadows, like beings from another dimension, dance on the stone walls, twisting and jerking to the beat from a hollowed log that mimics the very heart beat of the cavern. Leaping and flailing, the shadows appear to struggle within the walls trying to escape the cold, damp, darkness of their boulder bound bastion.

Barefooted hideously painted dancing men spawn the monster-like shadows. They adorn themselves with fangs, bones, and teeth from creatures such as the saber tooth tiger, the giant ground sloth, and the short-faced bear. All of these men have powerful, muscular bodies. Usually they are simply dirty and hairy, but on this day, paint, soot, and other types of stain and dye smeared their bodies and primitive wardrobes. Without intention, they cast their shadows upon the walls as they dance like the monsters they resemble.

The river flowing at the base of the bluff, with its raging central current, seemed too dangerous for travel. Yet, from that watery highway two men appear, arriving by an unsophisticated raft. Their search for this particular bluff has concluded. They have succeeded in finding the place they have only heard about in stories told around campfires in their homeland. The pulsing light served as their beacon.

One of these men is a thin man with a dark short beard. He is known by his clansmen as a thinker and explorer. His surviving team member is taller by half a foot and broader across the shoulders. He is known by his clansmen as someone very good to have on your side in difficult situations. They look about nervously as they pull their raft onto shore and secure it. Immediately they poise to defend themselves from any beast wanting to claim them for a meal. Three other members of their group have already been lost in that fashion in previous months. But still, they are a unified team of explorers, they work together to find the truth behind the stories. Walking toward their destination, lightning strikes close and thunder hammers the land. They jump instinctively and find themselves standing in mud, unaware of the link to the future they are making.

Proceeding more quickly toward the pulsing amber light coming from the rocky wall, they pause only momentarily at the base of the ladder before climbing to the mouth of the cave. They look at each other and ask silently, are you ready? Entering the jagged mouth of the opening, they emerge into the cavern and are amazed by its size and the activities going on.

Stepping into the light-filled cavern, they notice an earthen mound topped by a throne fashioned from large stones near the fire. Sitting on it with the dignity of royalty was an older, white-haired man. A deep scar marked his face from forehead to chin obliterating his left eye. Other signs of physical mishap lay covered by his clothing, yet those scars and bite marks bare testimony to the courage and tenacity he has demonstrated in his life. Though a recluse, he is known as a wise man, sought after for his words of wisdom and inspiration. He has summoned this gathering and has asked the spirits for the storm creating a mystical, more impressive atmosphere.

Momentarily distracted from his concentration into the fire, he notices the two newcomers enter and recognizes a kindred soul in the thin man, even though they have never met.

He returns his stare into the leaping, dancing flames, allowing himself once again to be mesmerized by the chaos of the inferno at his feet. The dancers and the dancing flames moved as if the will of the old man was imposed upon both. He nodded his head in silent understanding at the similarity. He appears both powerful and mystical. Though his right hand is missing one finger, his grip was strong upon a long, immaculately decorated staff fashioned from the bone of some large creature. The images carved into the staff depicted scenes of savage encounters that had been essential to his development and position.

Normally the old man's single eye was a wide-open dark well. But now it had narrowed to focus on a spot in the flames that no one could see but him. Unblinking he watched the fire, seeing beyond the frantic inferno. He realized again the connection between the fire, the sun, and the white hypnotic blend of these mystical lights that opened a door in his mind, creating a passage to unlimited knowledge.

Sitting regally upon his throne, he is incapable of suppressing a natural exhibition of strength, inner peace and eternal wisdom, marking him as a Shaman. He captured and held the respect of every man dancing around the fire. To bring this dancing frenzy to its climax, he stands raising his staff. Then he rapped it firmly on the ground at his side. The dancing stopped abruptly; they turned as one to listen to his impending oration.

The savages clutched their spears and bone clubs as they watched the old man with anticipation. The narrowed eye of the Shaman peered through the flames, searching the faces of his nervous followers. They were simple people, easily frightened. Except for one he noticed, the new comer. The raging storm and the frenzy around the fire sharpened their senses creating in them an adrenaline overload.

The Shaman stood above the group, his brow furrowed in concentration. Fixing his one-eye stare on the thin, young newcomer, he recognized his search was over. Though he made an almost imperceptible nod of approval to himself, still he looked over the other men hoping to see the same recognition in their faces, but found them wanting.

With an unbelievable high pitch, the Shaman screamed out, "Skreeeee!" mimicking the call of an eagle. He began to dance as his tribesmen were doing, bellowing chants and acting possessed. The frightened savages unaware of the reasons for this sudden outburst jumped nervously, weapons at the ready.

The old man knew what he was doing; this act was a deliberate scare tactic to separate those with courage from the unworthy. The young man calmed the panic-stricken men and persuaded them to stand and listen as the Shaman's composure changed back to rigid silence. Recognizing their failure in a test of courage, the men hung their heads in shame and reluctantly resumed their positions around the fire.

The old man descended the steps from his elevated throne and walked over to the young man. The others shrank back several steps. The Shaman pointed to the fire then raised his hand and pointed to the opening of the cave. A bolt of lightning flashed as if on cue. The savages tightened their group and chattered nervously among themselves, yet the young man stood calmly, seemingly unconcerned by the show of power. The Shaman extended his hand palm up. Eager to touch, the young man reached out.

With their hands just a fraction of an inch from contact, a static electrical arc crackled between their fingers. Pulling back his hand, the young man looked at the Shaman with wonder. Then, throwing aside his caution, he quickly reached out and took the old man's hand with a tight grip. A surge of energy passed between them. Their bodies flexed involuntarily. Cool, refreshing, clearing air flowed through the young man's nostrils making him feel as if every pore in his body had opened to the flow. A sudden clarity of mind and sharpness of senses nearly overwhelmed him.

They squeezed each other's hand with a bone crushing grip. The young man had seen his own visions, though darkly, as if through a heavy fog, but he had never experienced anything like this. He felt wind clearing smoke from his eyes, but there was no wind; he felt water washing away dirt and debris, but there was no water. Yet, now, he could truly see!

The old man released the young man's hand, breaking the grip and the spell. The young man stepped away slowly, but remained closer than the other, now thoroughly frightened, men. He knew the Shaman was now ready to speak; and he wanted to hear every word.

They all listened as the old Shaman began to unfold the visions that have passed by the eyes of his mind. He knew that most, if not all of what he said to these men would not be understood. He told them knowing they would take these unbelievable words away then, through storytelling, sow these words like seeds upon others.

The group sat for hours listening to the old man. He spoke of dwellings like caves, level upon level, where clans of people lived. He talked about people moving over the land covering great distances, until the clans reached from horizon to horizon. The young man stood close, listening to each exciting vision.

Many times the crowd broke into spontaneous laughter as the Shaman tried to explain visions for which they had no references. They laughed uproariously when he told them men would ride flaming birds into the heavens, to visit and explore the bright specs of light that filled the night sky. Yet he kept to himself the visions even he did not understand. His lack of understanding, however, did not cause him to disbelieve. His evolutionary thought process, his ability to see what has yet to come, was the trait that set him apart from the others.

The storm outside passed. The sun broke through as the clouds thinned and moved away only an hour or so before sunset. The fire had burned itself down to a glowing pile of red embers.

The entire day had been spent dancing and listening to the old man. Now he fell silent and sagged under the weight of his robe. He sighed deeply. It was over. These men had seen and heard what he had gathered them for. It was entertainment for many, a ritual requiring attendance by others.

The thin, young newcomer, as the lone exception, had listened with interest and understanding to the old man throughout the course of the day.

The group was dismissed when the Shaman turned his back to them. Lighting a torch from the embers he carried it to a nearby wall where he set to work finishing a mural he had been working on for many days.

After the other men left, the young man walked with his companion to the mouth of the cave. They watched the others silently descend the ladder and disappear into the under growth. The sun slowly descended over the land that would, in another twenty thousand years, be called South Dakota.

Standing in the entrance to the cavern, the young man thought of the things the Shaman said and wondered how it would be possible for large groups of people to live permanently close together. He shook his head being confused.

He knew why their clans broke up when they reached a certain number; the land could no longer sustain their needs. Separating and moving on became a condition for survival. How could future people do anything else?

Looking down he contemplated a white patch of hair on his animal skin robe. He ran his fingers through it. The contrast of the white animal hair against the dark brown, almost blackness of his skin was stark. The wise old man said others would come. He said they would be white men and they would come from the water. He had come from the water but he wasn't white. This confused him even more. He had never seen nor heard of a person being white. He thought about this as he held his hand up and studied his dark flesh against the white hairs on the skin robe.

Looking over his shoulder he saw the old man still standing by the mural, working on it by the light of the torch he held. He watched as the old man put a few more touches of white chalky paste on the mural. The old Shaman stopped painting and turned to look at the young man once more. They nodded an unspoken acknowledgment to each other.

The young man turned to watch the sun as it dropped out of sight beyond the land. A rumbling of movement and the low growl of a stalking beast came to him from somewhere close by. Undistracted, he never turned his attention from the setting sun. Mesmerized, he recalled the old Shaman saying the white people would come across the great water from the direction of the rising sun. That statement also caused the others to laugh and doubt.

They laughed because they thought the light giving orb rose up out of the land. They also believed it set into some hidden hole as it dropped out of the sky. Curious individuals set out to find the holes where the light orb rose from and set into. They were never seen or heard from again.

This thin young man and the old Shaman knew where the sun came from and where it went after the day was over.

He shook himself free from the thought of others not being able to see what was clearly before them and refocused on his mission.

The river he and his companion navigated was the mission. They wanted to find out where the river originated. Other explorers from his clan departed soon after he and his expedition members left, going in the opposite direction, to find out where it went.

As he thought about these things he became captive to a blend of light emanating from the setting sun. The eyes of his mind could see the answers to all his questions. He saw the white man. He saw him as an explorer like himself, searching for answers.

The sun dipped below the horizon compromising the formula, breaking the spell of the mystical light blend.

Closing the door in his mind, the vision retreated. Limited though the message had been, he had seen it and knew it meant he and the old Shaman were two of a kind.

CHAPTER ONE

The sun shone brightly as it slowly tracked across the clear blue sky. Throughout the day, not a single cloud offered members of the Lewis and Clark Expedition the slightest relief from the intense glare and heat. It was late afternoon; the sun would continue to burn the land for several more hours.

The expedition members were surprised but delighted when Captains Lewis and Clark decided to stop for the day. It was at least several hours sooner than they normally would have stopped. Their reasons being the heat had stressed everyone. That was certainly true. But it was also true that they had been stressed by the heat several other times before without sympathy from the Captains. They had been traveling along a waterway the Lakota Indians called, the *Mni Shoshe*. Later in history this waterway will be called The Missouri River. Captain Meriwether Lewis had become so captivated by a natural image of beauty he just had to confer with his co-leader, Captain William Clark. He pleaded with him to agree to give an order to stop for the day.

"My dear friend, just behold this magnificent, inspiring scenery." Captain Lewis said nearly overwhelmed with excitement. Their keel boat and small fleet of canoes slowly approached a monolith of a bluff. Every person present stared up in awe at the spectacle of a natural monument. The river acted like a mirror and reflected the image of the monolith as their flotilla slowly moved closer.

Captain Clark needed no invitation to be inspired. He had been captured by the same mystical power that his counterpart had been captured by. Unable to refrain from giving the order, William Clark shouted out a command, "put ashore and make camp." Sacajawea, the Shoshone Indian woman on the expedition, said this place had great mystical powers.

Joseph and Rubin Field are brothers who were recruited by Meriwether Lewis for the expedition. Lewis confessed to them upon their first meeting that he received a strong spiritual impression from them.

He said, "Something mystical, something telling my soul that you two are needed here, I really don't know why but it has something to do with a vision I had."

Lewis finished by saying. "Please don't be frightened, I am a sane man and am the personal secretary of our president, Mr. Thomas Jefferson. I am recruiting men of high quality to make history and to also make a better path for our nation and for all of humanity to grow on."

They were convinced to join the expedition after hearing more about the reasons, the challenge, and the compensation.

Another member of the team served as Captain Clark's personal servant prior to and during the expedition. He too, was more than happy to be part of this expedition. But he had another reason for participating. He was told he would be a free man upon completion of the journey. His name was York.

William Clark could have easily done without the aid of his servant on this mission. But a vision of future events gave him reason to recruit York.

"You do not have to accept this invitation." Clark said to him. "We might well be on our way to our demise. The land we'll be traversing is on no map. I am not ordering you to go."

Lewis and Clark agreed that York was destined to be a part of the expedition for reasons that would only be known and understood to future generations. They couldn't agree how or why they thought so. They only believed that it should be.

Rubin and York were chopping and gathering firewood together when the captain called out, "Mr. Rubin."

"The Captain is calling for me York. I got to go see what he wants." Rubin handed his axe to York and hurried away.

Captain Clark was sitting on a large stone and reviewing the notes in his journal when Rubin presented himself. "Yes sir?"

"I want you to find our Captain Lewis please." The tone of this request came more from one friend to another, rather than like the hard orders that were given to the other men.

Rubin was the only person, other than Captain Clark, that Meriwether Lewis had bonded with. It may have been because Captain Lewis had a step-brother named Rubin, or because Rubin had an outgoing personality that few persons disliked.

Maybe it was because Rubin seemed to empathize with the Captain's constant struggle with mood swings. Whatever the reason, Rubin was always called upon to communicate and watch over the often troubled Captain Lewis.

"Where is our captain?" Rubin asked, turning his head to look around dramatically in all directions.

Pointing in the general direction along an obscure path Captain Clark answered. "I last saw him back that way, maybe a half mile or so." The Captain tried hard to suppress a smile at Rubin's exaggerated look into the distant landscape.

The team had grounded their keel boat and canoes at a landing point near the base of a bluff. An auspicious landing sight, they chose it for the feeling it radiated. Immediately upon landing all members of the expedition stood in quiet awe at the sight before them.

Looking up the rise of the monolithic bluff, Sacajawea, the Shoshone Indian woman — the only female on the expedition — remarked, "This place has great mystical power; we are all supposed to stay for the night and give thanks for our good fortune."

Chosen members of the team spread out to find and make a comfortable, safe place to camp for the night. The military agenda included securing and posting a defensive perimeter around the camp. This was after all, an unknown land rumored to be inhabited by the much feared Lakota Indians. They have already had some trouble and feared they might have to shoot their way out of a tense situation weeks earlier. Yet Captain Lewis, despite the danger, had taken notice of something interesting on the ground immediately after their landing and began an impromptu exploration.

Rubin nodded his head, understanding the order given. He gave a little salute that might have seemed contemptuous in another military situation, but he got away with it here.

Captain Clark studied Rubin. Smiling he added, "You'll have to look for him, you know." Rubin cocked his head, wondering what had not been said in that statement and what was lurking behind the presumptuous smile of the Captain. "You may have to look down." He was pointing down to the ground. "You could pass him by and not even know it. I saw him looking at some fossilized tracks. I'm afraid he's allowed himself to get too caught up in this endeavor. Please watch over him."

Rubin noticed a slight tone of concern in the Captain's request. Lewis and Clark had been friends for years and the respect and affection they had for each other was obvious.

Rubin pointed his thumb at himself and said, don't worry, sir. I'll find him." He turned on his heels and strode away.

Captain Clark called after him, "Just watch over him and keep him company please."

Rubin understood. He waved over his shoulder without turning to face Captain Clark. Another contemptuous, yet harmless act only Rubin got away with.

Less than a half mile down the path, Rubin found the very studious captain down on his hands and knees studying something on a stone surface. The Captain looked up when he heard Rubin approach. "What ya got there, Captain?" Rubin asked. He scanned the area carefully before he allowed his defenses to relax.

"Come down here and get a better look," the Captain said, as he repositioned himself. He sat back on his rump as he stretched his legs out in front of him with a sigh of relief.

Rubin knelt down and studied what looked like human footprints in the stone. "What do you think of this," Captain Lewis said as he waved his hand along a fossilized path. He had taken great care in clearing away debris that had for ages covered the tracks.

Rubin touched the footprints. "Is this what it looks like?" The Captain nodded his head vigorously.

"Are these really footprints of people?" Rubin asked. "Yes, they are Rubin. People have been here before us." The Captain proclaimed with certainty. "And they're in stone," he said softly, nodding his head joyfully.

"That means they are at least ten thousand years old, maybe much older I really can't be certain," Captain Lewis proclaimed. Rubin looked dumbfounded. "The direction of this ancient trail leads straight along this path and goes someplace up there." He motioned toward the stone face of the steep bluff only a few yards away. "Let's have a look."

Walking slowly, they carefully explored the path to the bluff, searching for clues to anything. Several other footprints were seen indicating the direction, yet they seemed to stop right at the base of the stone monolith.

"Now what do ya suppose happened here?" Rubin asked, looking around. Captain Lewis didn't respond. He could see a pile of stones about forty feet up on a catwalk-like edge. "Let's get up there." He said urgently.

They cut and lashed two slender trees together for a makeshift ladder. Though wobbly and springy, it worked. Upon reaching the ledge they found it piled with fallen stones. They paused to survey the area. There was still several hours left before the sun would set, enough time for exploration Lewis believed. From their vantage point, they could see the rest of the expedition members through the thin canopy of treetops. They saw Sacajawea leaning over the campfire, cooking and hurrying about as her husband sat and watched without helping in the least. Her baby, Pomp, was lashed to a cradle board and leaned against a rock, always close to her.

The captain muttered in a low tone. "She's a remarkable woman." Rubin nodded his head in silent agreement. "She deserves more than that Frenchman she's with," Captain Lewis added with a venomous tone.

The Captains, as well as the crew, had developed a negative attitude toward her husband, Charbonneau. He was hired as a guide, a translator and cook. He wasn't good at any of the three. And after a mishap in a canoe that caused the loss of some critical equipment, a mishap attributed directly to him, he was now considered a dangerous liability. Captain Clark had to threaten Charbonneau at gun point to paddle his canoe and try to salvage some of the lost equipment. Rubin and the Captain returned their attention to the pile of stones. The Captain was first to notice something out of place. Though his mind whirled as he made observations, he found himself focusing on the pile of rubble. They looked like they were stacked and piled, not fallen as they had looked from below. "Let's move a few of these stones," he said.

Working fast, they soon uncovered an opening into a cavern. "Just as I thought!" Lewis exclaimed. Rubin almost expected him to clap his hands and dance on the narrow ledge. Looking into the dark recess, he said with excitement, "We'll need torches. Please hurry back to camp and bring something we can use to light our way." Rubin nodded and hurried away.

Returning with several torches lashed to his back, Rubin said, "I told Captain Clark we were exploring a cavern. He made me promise we'd return soon."

"You're a good man, Rubin," the Captain replied, putting his hand on Rubin's shoulder. Then quickly striking flint to steel, he ignited the precious soft rodent nesting material they all carried in small pouches and used as tinder for starting fires. Applying the small flame to the torches, their oil-soaked heads quickly burst into flame.

As they cautiously walked into the cavern, the sun at their backs, their shadows cast monster-like images upon the walls. Rubin ignored the visage and instead looked around the room. "Over there, Captain. Those stones have been stacked like a chair or something." Rubin said, pointing to the carefully piled rocks. "What do you suppose that was for?"

Captain Lewis moved to the stacked stones and touched them reverently not replying to Rubin's comment. His wonder consumed him completely. Holding his torch up high, he looked around. Rubin followed his example. They both paused and stared at one of the walls. "What have we here?" Captain Lewis asked quizzically.

Stepping closer, Rubin said, "It looks like a picture of some sort." The ancient mural was plain to see in the torch light, virtually unmarred by time in the sealed cavern.

Captain Lewis closely studied the images in detail while Rubin continued to look around. Returning his attention to the stone chair, Rubin realized it was most likely a throne. Walking over to it, he sat down.

The entire interior of the cavern could be seen from his vantage point. A large fire pit lay at his feet.

Beyond the fire pit he could see through the opening of the cavern. The setting sun lay before him. He asked himself if maybe this throne of stones was erected in this exact spot so the seated person could watch the sunset. As he watched, a peaceful, calm feeling began to spread over him.

And as the sun dropped lower in the sky, a beam of sunlight slowly aligned onto Rubin's face. He couldn't look directly at the sun without squinting his eyes. But now, as he sat on the thrown, with the sun rays beaming into his eyes, he saw an assortment of yellows, oranges and reds. These sun rays blended into a white light that entered his eyes and illuminated his imagination.

The white light grew in his mind, bringing images of things foreign and unknown. An image of falling rain and people searching for something clearly formed in the eye of his mind. He realized his vision was similar to what he and the others of the expedition were doing: searching for knowledge in unfamiliar lands and places.

Suddenly he found himself standing in the opening of the cavern, not remembering moving from the throne, but obviously, he had. Nearly forty feet above ground level, the view inspired him. Looking down, a living portrait of life slowly passed before his eyes. His soul had become captive to a natural force invoking a sense of *Karma*, a peaceful emptiness. The day was ending as he stood watching.

Captain Lewis touched him on the shoulder, jolting him from his trance, shattering his deep thoughts.

"They knew," he whispered. "They could see." Rubin cocked his head quizzically at the Captain's remark and facial expression. The Captain looked as though he had just seen or heard something unbelievable. It scared Rubin. Looking back into the cavern, Rubin expected to see a ghost. He was about to ask who knew what, but a deep commanding voice jolted him again, interrupting his thoughts.

"Ya'all best be coming back to da camp; it gettin' on dark." It was York, his head just above the edge of the rock ledge. Standing on their makeshift ladder, he had come to take them back to camp.

The walk to camp was slow and quiet. Rubin didn't want to ask questions yet. He could tell Lewis was in deep thought, as often he was. Rubin also understood the Captain's need for quiet meditative times to sort things out, in particular after a discovery such as the one they just made.

In the past, Rubin and Meriwether shared long conversations about social issues, politics, religion and economics. Rubin knew he was in the presence of a highly educated man. Then one day Meriwether said to him, "Try to understand how I feel since I have learned certain things. I've been aware since early childhood that the world is rapidly changing. I also observed many times throughout my life that changes in life require more changes of life. Nothing ever stays the same. A professor once told me that is what cause and effect are. Something changes that requires other things to change. I believe some people were created to change, maybe even control the chaos that is the code of life. Others of course are involved, volunteering as workers for progress and stability. Would not these perceptions of life cause you to be just a bit concerned, maybe even depressed?"

Rubin knew this was just one of many explanations in which Captain Lewis rationalized with his mood swings. He also knew the Captain would, in his own time and in his own way, explain what he had seen and what he meant when he said, "They knew." Meanwhile, in his own mind, he kept seeing that almost-hypnotic blend of light radiating from the sun, hiding in plain view.

CHAPTER TWO

Rubin immediately shared his experience in the cavern with his brother. Long discussions followed. Sky watching became an obsession to them for the duration of the trip. Now back in St. Louis, they've chosen a hill just outside of town for their evening meditations and observations, watching for the elusive hypnotic blend of light.

On the western horizon, streaks of orange and crimson accented the fading yellow of the setting sun. From the east, shades of blue forced the color festival of the sun to retreat. Rubin and Joseph watched the sunset together as they had almost every evening since their return to St. Louis one month before.

They were trying to recapture and hold the essence of the magic feeling they discovered while they explored with Lewis and Clark. Rubin was convinced, after his experience in the cavern, that a formula existed that could open the mind of a person to the flow of universal knowledge. A piece of the procedure, he believed, consisted of a pattern of light combinations. Joe had no experience with this incredible perception but believed his brother. Together they searched for the blend of light that was supposed to be a key ingredient to this formula. Joe closed his mind to nothing.

The sun set over the land they called Eden. They missed being there. It was a land of honor and dignity, challenge and conquest over personal limits. Upon the hilltop, Rubin and his brother sat in silent reverie. A command from somewhere deep within their souls held them captive. They barely noticed a pair of birds flying across their view of the sinking orange orb, far out in the distance.

"What do you suppose is going on out there now," Rubin asked softly.

"It's still daylight out there you know. I suppose their preparing for night, like most people do. Hobbling their horses and stacking enough fire wood for the night" Joseph answered as he puffed on his pipe.

Eventually, the sun surrendered the sky to the deepening blue from the east. They held their gaze as the last few seconds of mystical twilight blended into darkness. Chirping crickets officially declared the beginning of night. The trance they had fallen into was slow to relinquish the control it had on them. But tonight, the soft blend of light did not appear.

Dim lights flickered as the city tried to illuminate itself and remain viable into the night, struggling to prolong activity. Retirement for the night and an effort to conserve energy were not considered by most. They pay no heed to the city.

A chill was in the air. Rubin shivered, Joseph pulled his jacket together tightly across his chest. This evening, a Friday in October 1806, was much like other evenings they had spent since their return in September. The peace and quiet acted as a form of meditative therapy to them.

This time and place marked the end of their day, a time to reflect on their constantly changing life. They recently heard about an insurgence planned for the west and about a pastor, with a small congregation in St. Louis, named Ross. They were concerned about his determination to make a pilgrimage west to convert the Indians to Christianity. The peace and happiness Rubin and Joseph expected to enjoy for the rest of their lives had now become elusive. Summer, with all its lively activities, has ended, and the end of the seasonal life cycle of nearly all plant life. The cool air, the smell of tannin from the fallen leaves, the early sunset, all worked in harmony to trigger a mood of resignation.

Other information recently learned has given them reason to doubt the intent and sincerity of the federal government they had worked for these past two years. They can no longer see hope for the future. Instead, the developing American culture no longer reflected what they believed the early leaders envisioned for the infant nation of America.

As leaves rustle in a gentle breeze, memories of events from the expedition sailed past their eyes, causing doubt and dread to overwhelm them. Joseph's voice, normally strong and commanding, was soft, almost inaudible. Still, it rang in Rubin's ears as if it were shouted. *"My God, what have we done?"*

They had no words to define their feelings. Slowly they gathered themselves and headed back home. As they walked, Rubin asked Joseph, "Do you think any of the discoveries we made on the expedition will cause trouble for the Indians, or our country?"

"Men kill for gold," Joseph answered. "And you know how some trappers over harvest beaver pelts. Silver is growing in demand also. Yes, I believe most of the mineral discoveries we made will cause trouble for our Indian friends. Prospectors will flood their lands."

"I want to believe natural resources would not be used to lure people into prospecting," he concluded with a worried tone.

Trying to sound convincing but failing, Rubin added. "I'm confident treaties will protect the Indians and their land."

Joe laughed knowing about too many broken, violated treaties.

"I hate to say this, but we need to go back," Joseph proclaimed!

Rubin stopped walking and with a raised voice said, "Go back? You mean . . . everywhere we visited before?"

"All the Indian camps, at least. We need to warn them about these new developments."

Joseph raised his tone a bit and sounded urgent. "They'll lose their land! They'll lose their way of life. We must go back. The white man is coming and it can't be stopped."

They stood in the darkness looking at each other contemplating the seriousness of the situation. They began to feel as though they had been used as unwitting accomplices. Using them to put into motion a program that would someday cause the demise of the Native Americans they had met, and now considered friends. There didn't appear to be any deliberate attempt to destroy the Indians, not at that point anyway, but they could see it as a possible side effect of poor policies and practices and overriding greed. Shame and anger filled their thoughts. They prayed they were wrong, but feared they were not.

"Well I guess we better put together a plan." Rubin said with a deep sigh.

Rubin and Joseph worried not only for all the Indians they had met, but for others they had only heard of. One such secret tribe was known as *The Wooesa*. They were considered a sacred group, known by other Indians as a clan radiating compassion and love. Above all, they were noted for bringing warring parties together in lasting peace.

A *Wooesa* wasn't born from *Wooesa* parents. A person became a *Wooesa* after attaining a certain level of spiritual awareness setting them apart from other people.

Though a true *Wooesa* never claimed to have mystical powers, it was apparent they did indeed have some kind of connection to the spirit world. Some claimed *The Wooesa*, like prehistoric Shamans, could even see into the future.

A *Wooesa* made war with no one, and no Indians made war with them. They spoke of and lived a simple life that was harmonious, in as much as was possible, with nature. Troubled people could find peace and a more meaningful way of life after being in their company for just a short amount of time. They were said to practice rituals that would take a person's soul to *The*

Creator's door. And it was said that after this visit with *The Creator*, a person was incapable of living a troubled life. These Indians brought peace while evoking a higher level of consciousness in those who would listen.

Yet these people remained elusive, hiding in plain sight, only showing themselves to intervene when absolutely necessary. People sought them out, but only the worthy could find them. It was people such as this that Pastor Ross considered a big threat to his religious beliefs.

CHAPTER THREE

Joseph is the oldest brother. His face is marked with deep wrinkles and there are stress furrows on his brow, testimony to the hard life he has lived.

His beard, now tipped with gray, and his hair, turning white around the ears, were once dark brown. He is a robust man and assumed a fatherly role at an early age after their father failed to return home from one of his many trips. Those excursions had taken weeks at a time, sometimes as much as a month, and had been understood and accepted by his family as part of his job as a government surveyor and map maker.

Yet no one ever really knew what happened to him. It could have been Indians, pirates, illness, or a wild animal attack. The only thing certain was, he never returned home. Joseph tried to step into those vacated shoes.

Joe is a very philosophical, patient, and tolerant man. His constant concerns for his family, community, and country have taken a toll though, making him look older than his thirty-one years. He refers to Rubin as the pup.

Rubin is the youngest son, and youngest brother at twenty-two years old. A permanent smile on his face, a bright outlook on life, and an ever-present sense of humor define him. He is a bit shy, especially around pretty women. Ladies have been heard to say he would be a great find for the right woman.

And there is Gustove, the brother in the middle, twenty-six years of age, and the only one of the three who is married. He has a bit of Joseph's serious maturity tempered with a bit of Rubin's youthful humor. He and his wife Rachel are loved and respected by his brothers and community members. The plan he has for their future revolved around her. They have agreed to live close to his brothers and hope to have several children.

Gus is less idealistic and a little more realistic than Joseph. He is more domestic than his siblings and was always close to his mother. He was a married man at the time of the recruiting, making him ineligible to participate with the expedition. Joe and Rubin are brother figures in the eyes of Gus and is a confidante to both. Joe and Rubin have a different relationship between themselves, theirs being more like father and son.

As Joe and Rubin struggle with the dilemma of knowing two different cultures are destined to crash together, Gus struggles with his own culture divide, getting his married legs under him. Privately Joe and Rubin wondered in amazement at their brother being married to a beautiful woman who wanted to be with him and have his children. There were times they envied him.

Gus had confided to Rachel how amazed and proud he was of his brothers who were living legends. They had become historically known as explorers and adventurers. There were times he envied them.

One day Gus confided to Joe, "I love her and want her to be happy. But I'm afraid the course we've chosen for our lives will be too hard. I don't want to see her sad or unhappy."

Joseph had great control of his emotions. Gus never even suspected he raised the ire of his brother with his statement. Joe calmly lit his pipe and gently but firmly chided him.

"Life is hard on everyone Gus. Sadness comes, sadness goes. You can't protect her from life; just remind her daily how happy you are that she has chosen to share life and all its hardships with you."

"You're a wise man Joe, thank you for those words. I guess I would do better if I looked at things differently."

Joe added, "If I could teach you one thing to remember it would be *the code of life*. Nothing is as bad as it seems and goodness is usually in balance with bad. And just one more note Gus, you have a wonderful woman with you. If you love her and she loves you, if you are both lost in time and oblivious to the world around you when you embrace, then you have reached the crowning achievement of life."

The words Joe spoke combined with the aromatic scent from his pipe tranquilized Gus. The dark fears and anxiety that had plagued him had been blown from his soul by the breath of his brother's wisdom.

Rachel is married to Gus. She makes him happy and keeps him content. She is his best friend, his companion, and one day yet to come, will be the mother of his children. He considers himself very fortunate.

Gus met her in 1798 when they attended a community meeting about a flood control project in St. Louis. They shared their ideas with people at an open meeting in town to discuss a reoccurring problem. Their points over the issues were sound and wise and caught the attention of the council members. Mr. Cecil Wilson was on the council and asked her, "How did you learn so much about drainage young lady?"

"I grew up in Philadelphia and we had more problems from poor drainage than we could deal with," she responded factually. Gus heard her answer and was dumbstruck.

"And where did you acquire your knowledge sir," he asked Gus politely?

"Well sir," he bulked for a moment being more concerned about seeing the lady he heard speak. He stood on toes and stretched his neck trying to get a look over the heads of people at this lady who said she came from Philadelphia.

"I too was born and raised in Philadelphia and I remember very well the problems we had from blocked drains in our streets." Mr. Wilson smiled broadly seeing two bright, young people who looked like they were without a spouse at their side.

With strong emphasis he said, "I believe you two may have been neighbors." He addressed the Crowd, "Please fellow citizens; let's allow these two young people to meet." From the center of the podium he motioned with his hands for the crowd to part. They did like water before Mosses.

Gus gasped as he looked upon a young lady who was the prettiest woman he had ever seen. He pulled the hat from his head but could not speak. He could only stare. Rachel blushed, and looked shyly away as she fidgeted with her bonnet strings.

Mr. Wilson saw the awkward situation he created and reacted quickly. He jumped down from the podium, walked quickly to the rear of the crowd and grabbed Gus by the arm. He walked Gus forward to where Rachel stood. She was now fanning her pink cheeks.

"What's yer name young man," Mr. Wilson asked. Gus had to think, and then he remembered. "Gus, my name is Gus," he said proud that he remembered his name.

There was laughter in the crowd as they gathered around the young couple, enjoying themselves at their expense.

"And what's yer name young lady," he asked Rachel respectfully. She looked at Mr. Wilson, not at Gus and said, "My name is Rachel Clemens." Mr. Wilson had a little fun with them and so did the rest of the crowd.

"Let me introduce you two to each other." He did and the crowd cheered. Gus greeted her with his hat in hand and a slight nod of his head.

Mr. Wilson applauded when they finally walked away with each other. He shouted at them as they departed the crowd assembly. "We'll take your suggestions under consideration." They were beyond seeing or hearing anybody or anything. They could only see and hear each other.

They chatted for a long time. Gus discovered that she and her family had been residents of Pittsburg while they were growing up also.

"Pa was a map maker for the government and was always being sent to a new frontier somewhere.

That's how we ended up here." He said. "We've been in St. Louis for ten years. Pa has been missing for nine and a half years." He concluded sadly.

Rachel held his hand as she confided in him. "Ma died almost four years ago of the pox. I remember crying and wanting to see her, but my Aunts kept me away. They said it was for my own good. Then one day they took me to her window so I could talk to her." Rachel started to sniff as tears dripped from her chin. Gus sat close and put his arm around her till she calmed.

He sniffed her hair. Her leg touched his. His breath became heavy. She looked up at him with tear filled eyes and cried out, "I miss my Mama!" He held her and whispered, "It's alright."

They sat together for a very long time without saying anything else. Then after she composed herself she resumed her story.

"After everything was over, Pa moved me and my two brothers here. That was almost four years ago."

They sat and looked into each other's eyes for a very long time. Gus felt his life changing.

Rachel turned out to be a supreme homemaker. She assumed her mother's domestic role upon her death and had become the lady of the house, fussing over and taking care of her father and two brothers. She was sixteen when her mother died, and now had the respect of the women who had taken her under their wings here in St. Louis. She could do things other women twice her age only thought about. They had taught her skills her mother didn't know, and explained many other things her father and brothers had no knowledge of.

Gus liked everything about her and knew without a doubt that she was the woman he had been waiting for while they were on an evening walk. They noticed a mare having difficulty bearing its foal as they strolled by a neighbor's barnyard. The mare was frantic and made sounds Gus would have sworn was a call for support from one female to another. The neighbors weren't home. Rachel took it upon herself to comfort and keep the mare company during her labor. Gus thought he noticed eye communication between her and the mare. The calming effect she had on the mare by her words and touch was astounding. He was almost certain two females of different species couldn't communicate each other this way, but what he witnessed made him reconsider his thought. He proposed to her soon thereafter.

CHAPTER FOUR

A narrow boardwalk lined each side of the crowed, litter strewn street. It had a gentle roll in the lay and it creaked with every step from every person who walked upon it. Mud from the street had encroached on the walk way and with each passing day it claimed new territory, overrunning the boards as they sank into the mire.

The awnings and roof tops swayed and rolled in motionless harmony with the board walk. Still, this creaking, rolling stretch of boards was better to walk on than the dirty, dangerous, often muddy street. Horses trod the muddy road, people stayed on the boardwalk except to cautiously cross to the other side, being extra careful where they stepped.

They had discussed detouring around the volatile heart of the city. It would have taken ten, maybe fifteen minutes longer. Yet darkness came early at this time of year, so they gave the suggestion little serious consideration. Daylight had now become a precious commodity, worth the effort and risk of making a rapid walk through the heart of town. They were short on time but were determined to seize the magic moment, yet caution was needed; too many ruthless characters stalked the streets of town looking for an easy victim.

Joseph, Rubin, and Gus made their way into town on the wavy, rickety boardwalk. Starting in the east at the river edge where they grouped together after work each day. They walked across town headed west. Their destination was the hilltop, and from there, on to their home.

The boardwalk they had to use wasn't much better than the street; it had its own kind of litter. Instead of horse manure and mud made from rain and horse urine, the boardwalk held sleeping vagrants, tobacco spit, staggering drunks, and more hustlers than a normal minded person would think possible. But at least there were no horses to step on your foot.

A broken foot made it almost impossible to take care of yourself. Sympathy for anyone in such a situation was unheard of.

It was Friday night. The work day and the work week had ended. Shops and other businesses were closing for the night, some for the weekend. Oil burning lamps began to brighten the windows, slowly and softly illuminating the shadow-cast city. Multitudes of these lamps saved the river side city of gray warping planks from the flood of darkness.

Ornate glass globes topped tall, immaculately adorned lampposts, each being lit by a team of two men in a horse drawn cart. They were strategically and evenly placed along the sides of the street. Many of them were like the board walk, roofs and awnings; they tilted at slight angles, this way and that. At one time they must have certainly been straight. The soft light gave this busy city and its residences a deceptive warm, hospitable look.

The scent from eating establishments cooking their signature dishes filled the air. Being a commercial river-front city meant an exceptional large number of high quality eatery choices. These dining establishments looked out of place in this rugged outpost of a city. But entrepreneurs had chosen wisely. Some of these establishments will last for generations.

Saloons were just beginning to acquire and entertain their evening clientele. The crowds would soon become drunk and unruly. Drinking, gambling and prostitution dominated the later hours of the night.

Deals of all sorts were being made and money would change hands. Gus considered the Friday night crowd to be unworthy so he kept himself and his wife away.

With so many ruthless, shady characters around and involved in so many things, he doubted if anything honest was going on. Still there were some good people here and they called the city their home. They would struggle for years to make this place they called home, safe and respectable.

Joseph and Rubin were given employment in town as a gift from the city council. Though the Field brothers had other plans for their future, they were in a situation of having to wait before their expedition settlements would be finalized. Rubin and Joseph now worked at jobs that had been hastily arranged by the elected officials for the benefit of their renowned citizens. Rubin was a shore man on the river for a local freight company loading and unloading barges, Joseph as a new councilman at-large.

Rubin insisted that he take the job on the river despite protests from council members who wanted their hero son to wear a better suit of clothes and stay away from the riffraff. But the job on the river front seemed to fit the strong, outgoing youth.

The members of the city council created Joseph's job for him even though there had been no councilman at-large before then. His natural ability to get to the heart of almost any problem and the passion he had for social and community structure, made the job a perfect match for him.

Gustove was busy working out the details of the estate he and his brothers had inherited from their mother. She died while Joe and Rubin were away.

Gus now had to dispose of the house and property if they were all going to move on. He was stunned but pleased to find out how much money a large home in the outskirts of St. Louis, Missouri brought. The money from this estate sale, combined with the money, land and livestock the government owed his brothers for time spent on the Lewis and Clark expedition, would establish them nicely somewhere else.

Viola Field told her boys to sell the property after her death and move someplace where it was more peaceful. Before their departure, she encouraged Joseph and Rubin to learn about life while they explored. "I hope you will find new meaning to life and allow your lives to be devoted to peace and honorable fulfillment." Viola was a woman who knew more than she allowed people to believe she knew.

Rubin and Joe were having a difficult time getting readjusted to life in the city. People had developed harsh attitudes about many things while they were gone. Patience and compassion were missing they thought. Things seemed to be getting out of control here. Gus forbade Rachel from going to town alone. He made this decision after he learned about rapes and thefts going on without arrests being made. Being a feisty girl, she could have argued about it, but being a wise woman, she played along to his protective behavior. They didn't plan on living there much longer anyway.

The brothers headed west down main street on foot. As they saw the sun dropping lower in the sky, they put more speed in their stride. Joseph and Rubin had for the first time in their lives become acutely aware of the difference in lifestyles and philosophies existing between Native Americans and the white Europeans from the east. Before the Lewis & Clark adventure, they had never seen Indians in their natural environment. The contrast between their culture and that of the Indians startled them. Virtues, values and customs of the Indians were radically different from the white culture.

Rubin and Joseph realized their lives could never be the same after living as they had in the previous two years with the men of the expedition. Many sights they saw inspired them. And several Indian encounters opened their hearts and minds.

They hadn't considered how much their attitude and perception of life would change upon their return, yet their lives had been irreversibly changed.

Gus was experiencing his life-altering experiences too; marriage became his lesson in diversity and compromise.

Close as they were, the three Field brothers shared conversations about views of their ever changing lives. Gus was intrigued by the story from the cavern. He listened over and over again to the tale of the hypnotic blend of light that would occur with just the right set of circumstances. He occasionally joined Joseph and Rubin on their walks to the hill top with anticipation.

On previous trips through town, the three had noticed several Indians who had become regular vagrants. One old Indian seemed to be pushed around and abused more than others. "He's probably picked on more because he's old and can't defend himself the way the younger Indians can." Joseph commented.

Also, a large number of citizens were unjustifiably angry and afraid of the Indians. Stories of abuses to settlers by Indians ran through town like a wild grassfire. Consequentially some citizens took any opportunity they could to inflict pain or humiliation on any Indian they saw. There were laws protecting Indians from abuse but, in St. Louis Missouri, in 1806, white people could get away with murder. And they often did.

The old Indian they had seen before was usually drunk and dirty. Anybody with a functioning nose could smell him from ten feet away. He was referred to as a derelict scalp collector, even though nobody had ever seen him take or even possess a scalp. Oddly enough, he kept the reputation and, though he never left town, the stories about his monstrous behavior kept growing ever more unbelievable.

Rubin had, on several occasions, pulled the old drunk from what would soon have escalated into a dangerous situation.

Today the old Indian had been pushed through the batwing doors of a saloon and right into a group of local thugs walking down the boardwalk.

"Hey, what's the matter with you?" exclaimed one of the cocky young men.

"Stinkin' heathen," another one hissed, as he pulled a large knife from his belt.

"Hold on there a minute," said a man who followed the Indian out the door. The Fields suspected him as the one who had pushed the old Indian. "Don't hurt him yet. I got to find out where the old coot got his gold."

More knives, and one pistol, appeared instantly. The Kentucky flintlock was a single-shot, .48 caliber weapon that stretched thirteen and a half inches long. Although a heavy pistol, most people carried two, in case the first failed to fire. If both misfired, they became a formidable club.

The men began pushing the Indian back and forth between them as they laughed. These young thugs were the sons of local businessmen, though they dressed like trappers and frontiersmen. It was, as Joseph called it, "cultural civilian camouflage." These boys knew nothing about trapping and very little about any other kind of work. They routinely took what they wanted, showing no respect for anyone or anything. They roamed the streets looking for any opportunity. They considered themselves immune to the law and, with their fathers' influence, they were.

"You smell worse than an old, wet dog," one of them remarked cruelly.

Simple robbery, with a little physical abuse, was about the only entertainment they could expect out of this victim. The old Indian was either too drunk or simply didn't understand English well enough to answer or effectively communicate. The gold nugget he presented in the saloon for his drinks had either been stolen or he had come by it honestly. Either way he would never tell where he got it, no matter what they yelled at him or how many times they hit him.

Realizing the futility of their assaults the group pushed the old Indian out into the street, still cursing at him. They laughed as they began to walk away. One of the young thugs cocked his head towards his friend to better hear what was being said to him. He began to smile sadistically. He stopped, turned and walked back to the Indian. "I'm sick and tired of you filthy

Indians getting in our way and giving our town a bad name." He paused for a long minute. His hatred-filled eyes burned as he built up his courage to do the unthinkable. The other thugs watched and encouraged him to show the Indian who owned the town.

"You can take yer secret of gold to hell with you." He pulled his gun from his belt, and, without provocation, fired into the back of the crawling Indian.

"No!" Rubin screamed. He and his brothers rushed the locals, even though they were outnumbered two to one. The locals drew their guns. The Field brothers didn't carry side arms. A shout rang out from across the narrow street. "I got my gun leveled at yer guts and the next man to move gets an ounce of lead." Everyone froze. No one even blinked an eye though Joe and Gus trembled at the thought of Rubin being blasted if he couldn't control himself.

The jangling spurs and the long heavy stride proclaimed the overbearing presence of Sheriff John Mason. "Let's break this up before someone gets into trouble," he ordered.

Rubin immediately turned on the sheriff. "Arrest those bastards," he shouted as he and Gus rushed to the aid of the Indian.

The sheriff noticed the Field boys were unarmed. He turned his gun toward the group of thugs. They tucked their guns back into their belts and acted as pleasant and cooperative as good citizens could. They chuckled and responded boyishly. "Gosh sheriff, we're sorry."

Joe jumped forward and seized that one by the shirt, pulling him up and off his feet.

"Easy does it, Joe," the sheriff commanded. "Let him go." Joe tossed the boy into his unsuspecting friends, knocking them all to the ground.

"You boys get on home and stay out of town for the night," the sheriff ordered.

"You can't let them get away with what they've done," Joseph challenged.

The sheriff glanced over to the dying Indian, and then turned his attention to Joe." I know you boys got a different idea about the way things should be since you've went away," He paused for a long moment as he studied the senseless act. "But things here are still the same." He looked back to the Indian and finished his heartless testament. "He's just an old Indian, worthless as a three-legged mule."

He spat on the ground and walked away.

Joseph shouted at the sheriff. "You're supposed to be a part of the solution." The sheriff stopped in mid-stride though he didn't turn around. "Instead, you're part of the problem." Joe finished. The sheriff lowered his head slightly as if in shame, then resumed his long stride and walked away.

CHAPTER FIVE

Rubin knelt beside the old Indian, cradled him in his arms and said, "we're gonna get ya some help." Gus and Joseph stood over them feeling powerless as they looked down upon the pair. Their faces involuntarily contorted at the sweet pungent scent of blood. Sounds of gurgling fluid filled their ears. Gus turned his head, afraid of getting sick.

They knew help wasn't coming. They also knew what the final outcome of this senseless act was going to be. One question remained: Would death come mercifully fast or brutally slow?

Any questions or doubts pertaining to their motives for returning to the land of the Indians had just been answered. More reasons were not needed. From this moment on, they were on a mission. The path they were destined to follow had just been clarified. Up until now this city and the people that inhabited its borders were their home and heritage. This incident made the separation complete. The people here had just slipped past the point of salvation. Warning the Indians of their looming peril had become vital.

The thought of some sort of justice for the man who did the shooting never entered their minds. This was St. Louis Missouri, it was 1806, and this was the farthest outpost of the new independent nation of America. Only the hardest, meanest, most dangerous and determined people came through here. Some stayed, some moved on, many died.

The law was clear and easily understood. Chinese and Indians were to be treated fairly and equitably. That was the law as it was written. The interpretation of fair and equitable treatment was up to a white male of European decent to say. The truth was, there is no justice here for Indians, and there wouldn't be for many years to come, none would find much help on the edge of the frontier.

Rubin carefully held the old Indian in his arms. The man seemed unbelievably frail and weightless. Like a child, Rubin gently cradled him. As he held the dying Indian, a mysterious sensation began to sweep over him. His ears began to ring, his skin tingled. He felt emotional, almost to the point of tears.

Yet it wasn't the Indian he felt like crying for. It was a way of life he knew was being lost, a path to peaceful living being detoured. Compassion and love were being murdered. The old Indian represented a culture, a life force that would soon be extinguished to make way for a new more harsh and cruel reality.

"We're gonna get ya some help, do ya understand?" Rubin repeated to him even though he knew no help was coming.

The Indian looked up into Rubin's eyes and studied him carefully. He didn't seem to be in any kind of discomfort, nor did he appear angry or resentful. He just looked at Rubin with a calm, peaceful expression on his face, even though the rattling, gurgling sounds coming from his mouth indicated his breathing to be labored.

The behavior of this Indian in the face of death was something the Field brothers had never before seen. They considered themselves, as did others who knew them, to have had more than the usual experience with Indians. However, this Indian revealed something new to them.

His eyes communicated a clear message saying, "Don't be alarmed, everything is as it should be, I regret nothing."

He began to speak in his native language to someone or something close and unseen. Rubin looked around thinking the Indian was talking to another Indian who had just walked up, but he saw no one.

The dying Indian had a faraway look in his eyes as he spoke.

Rubin gazed up at his brothers. "What's he saying?" he asked. They shook their heads slowly, not knowing.

Rubin again looked into the Indian's dark eyes. A sparkle in those moist eyes created a hypnotic blend of light. Rubin had been caught unaware and unprepared. The reflection in the gleam in the eyes of the Indian seized him. He gasped as he made the connection. It was at the opening of the cavern on the Lewis and Clark expedition. The emotion, the stress, and then the light, these things together triggered an opening into a vast emptiness where his soul and the soul of the Indian mingled.

Spellbound, he felt himself powerless against the unseen force. He fell into a black void and accelerated through total blackness. It terrified him. He felt like he was out of his body. His equilibrium and eyesight failed him as he tried to free himself from the grip of the unseen force and regain composer. He wanted to cry out for help, but could not. Just when he realized he was not falling but everything was flowing through him at an unbelievable rate, he was freed. His return to his surroundings was so sudden he nearly swooned. Gasping, he looked to his brothers; they looked at him with alarm and concern.

"Are you okay?" Joe asked.

"How about it brother" Gus asked. "I thought you was gonna faint or something. Rubin didn't speak, only nodded at them, a gesture to say he was all right.

The Indian smiled at him. Rubin was mystified to see what he thought to be clouds floating in the Indian's eyes. He lowered his head once again and looked closer, not believing what he was seeing. An eagle was soaring gracefully through the clouds showing upon the dark brown of his eyes. Rubin rubbed his eyes trying to wipe away the mystic vision.

A soft chant, short, repetitious, and soothing, flowed from the Indian's mouth. Rubin recognized the chant as an Indian death song. As he sang he reached up to touch Rubin's face with trembling fingers.

"You can see," the Indian said in perfect English. Astonishment flashed across their faces. Looking back and forth at each other, they tried to confirm if they had indeed heard what they thought they heard.

"You all can see," the Indian said.

Beginning to struggle in his final minutes of life, he glanced between the brothers and repeated, "You all can see." He said with a trembling smile. "*The Seers of Maka* wait for you. Go to them. They will calm your troubled lives and help you see with the eyes of your soul, they are known as," He stiffened slightly and with great difficulty said "*The Wooesa.*"

"See what, what will we see, and what's a *Wooesa?*" Rubin begged. The Indian laughed softly, coughed lightly, and then expelled his last breath while Rubin peered deeply into his eyes. He jerked nervously when he heard the soft delicate cry of an eagle and saw, what he believed was, in the Indian's dying eyes, an eagle soar above the clouds and out of sight.

"Did you see that? Did . . . did you hear that," Rubin exclaimed. Gus and Joe shook their heads confused.

"See what?" Joe asked. "Hear what?" Gus followed.

Rubin sat cradling the now dead Indian and watched as a faint but distinct smile slowly set permanently on his lips.

A dark figure lurked in the shadows and had been watching and listening carefully. He had taken cover during the shooting and stayed hidden after.

The eavesdropper remembered hearing Reverend Andrew Ross rail against Indians and their savage beliefs on his street corner pulpit on week days. He knew where the ramshackle church of Reverend Ross was and knew he would want to know of these "*Wooesa.*" He smiled as he thought there might even be a little money in it for him if he included the Field brothers as a possible way to find these wayward Indians! He slipped away to relay his news to Reverend Ross.

It was late when they stood at the Indian's grave site. They had wanted to take the poor soul far away from town and build a burial rack aboveground, but it was too late at night. Hoping to save the old man from further molestation, they buried him in an unmarked grave.

"He would understand," Joseph said. "He would also be grateful we put him here by the river.

"Joseph added a few reverent phrases. He hoped his words, along with his brother's sincere feelings of remorse, would suffice for a service. He needed and wanted to do more, but this was all he and his brothers could do.

Rubin could not stop wondering about the sight he knew he saw in the Indian's eyes. The plunge into the blackness of somewhere unknown terrified him. He kept asking his brothers, "What is a 'Wooesa? Who are the 'Seers of Maka' and why would they be waiting for us?"

The moon was low on the edge of the horizon. They didn't have to look up very much to find themselves staring at the bright white orb. From behind them came the soft sounds of the distant city.

Joseph bit down on his pipe as he clenched his fist. Gus became transfixed by the reflection of the moon on the river and fell rapidly into a somber mood.

Rubin took notice and quickly intervened. "Be careful, it's the blend of light we've talked about." He pointed to the reflection of the moon on the river. "It doesn't have to come directly from the sun or moon; it can come from almost anywhere. Be careful, your emotions and the light can take you away." Gus looked at him doubtfully.

"Don't look at me like that; I'm trying to warn you. That's a passage." He pointed to the reflection of the moon on the river again.

"Emotions and a true sense to do something right, something good, and the light. These things together can take you away to a place that will make you believe you are falling through the air."

Gus asked concerned. "Rubin, what are you talking about?"

Rubin wanted to answer but suddenly realized a person must be spiritually open before they can be touched the way he had been.

"OK, I Think it's safe for you to look," he finally said. "Pay me no mind Gus; I've been different since the expedition. I see differently and I hear differently. I think maybe you cannot be affected the same way I am."

Gus nodded his acceptance of Rubin's explanation of his behavior. He saw a difference in Joe also.

Joe hadn't made excuses or explanations for his changed behavior. Joe was still analyzing all he learned.

The event of this day made him even more distant. Gus wondered quietly if the plans they all made to be together were going to be changed.

Joseph, Gus, and Rubin never intended to stay and live in St. Louis. They had plans to move far away from this kind of civilization. When their mother's estate would be settled, Gus would take his wife Rachel to a new homestead while Joseph and Rubin returned to the Indian nation.

They would all settle close together with adjacent lands after Joe and Rubin came back from their new mission. Rubin and Joe knew they had to do something to try and correct the problem they helped create before they could settle down. The problem they helped create was making it known that the west was rich with natural resources. Joe cringed every time he reminded himself that he and Rubin helped to make maps of where their discoveries were.

"We should have known better," he said in a low tone.

Development of a modified canoe and procurement of supplies topped their list of things to do. It would keep them busy all winter long. Yet, timing the departure to coincide with seasonal weather was something they could only pray for.

Their previous trip with Lewis and Clark was believed by themselves to be a once in a lifetime event. They were right about that. They believed the trip and the lessons they learned while on it would serve them personally and be beneficial to the fledgling nation also. They were right about that too.

But it has now become clear that *destiny* was *then* preparing them for another trip to the West, *now.*

"I feel privileged to be a torch carrier for humanity." Joe told Rubin. We have been chosen for some unknown reason to be able to see, hear and feel differently than most people." He added emphatically.

"We must try at any and all cost to plant a seed, a seed that will grow in the souls of all good people of this land. The fruit of that seed will be compassion."

They were experienced and knowledgeable enough to carry themselves through. Their new mission, to make contact once again with the Native Americans; and take to them another message, different from the one they presented when they were with Lewis and Clark. This time they would warn them of dire changes they foresaw.

A dominant spiritual theme among all Native American clans they encountered sparked their curiosity. Unintentionally they became spiritual men due to their exposer to these clans while away. The beginning of their spiritual exposer was with the discovery of the bluff and its contents. That incident opened Rubin's eyes to another world, another way to live. Now they hoped to return to these people, once referred to as subhuman but now known to Rubin and Joseph as equals, to help save their lives.

The informant carried his message to Andrew Bartholomew Ross. He carefully relayed the message.

"*The Wooesa,* you say?" Ross asked the informant.

"And they are spiritual leaders?" the informant added, laughter in his voice.

"Yes and the locals say they can talk to *God* and, through some kind of ceremony, help others to see and talk." he said in a cavalier tone.

Reverend Ross to *God* exploded with rage. "No one but we, who have been chosen and are worthy can commune with *God*! Do you understand?" His eyes turning red with rage! Spit flew from his lips as he yelled. "Those savage animals have no idea!"

The informant turned and fled, fearing the angry Reverend Ross. Andrew Bartholomew Ross fell to his knees, his hands clasped before him, praying out loud. I shall bring these heathens to You, Christ, or I will send them to hell!"

CHAPTER SIX

It was May, 1807. Long discussions and preparations had been made. Joe and Rubin were ready to go back to the land Lewis and Clark called "Eden." They would revisit and warn the Indians about what was really going to happen. Not the message of a peaceful co-existence brought by Captains Lewis and Clark, but a message of dire consequences.

Gus stood beside Rachel with his arm around her waist, holding her close, much closer than normal. She could sense his nervousness. After looking into the eyes of Joseph and Rubin, she concluded they were all apprehensive. That surprised her. "These seasoned explorers are actually reluctant to say goodbye," she thought. A giggle nearly slipped out. Her heart ached for them all, but mostly for her husband. He would be without his brothers once again.

Rubin and Joseph would have each other and would be out there somewhere sharing another adventure. Their first separation had been for a different reason. This time they were going to warn and prepare the Indians for a challenging future. And, upon their return, they would be reunited and be well on their way to the life they planned together.

She and Gus looked for a long time into the eyes of Rubin and Joseph. The prolonged silence spoke volumes. Rachel stepped forward to hug each of her husband's brothers long and hard.

"Take care. We'll be waiting for your return." She said with a trembling voice. She had spoken these words before. More than three years ago, she, her husband, and her mother in-law, Viola Field, said goodbye to Rubin and Joe. That had been a happier situation then.

Their outlook on life had been so much better when they were about to explore with Lewis and Clark. Now they were hopelessly disillusioned over all they had learned this past year.

There would be no compensation of land or money for this expedition. The benefit, if any, would be for future generations. The Field family would be the only investor in that future. They conceded after careful consideration that the dramatic change they prophesized would take place, only after several generations had past.

She turned, breaking away from the reassuring embrace of her husband. She quickly kissed Joseph, then Rubin, on the cheek. She ran to the waiting surrey, her tears were in full flow. Their horse softly whinnied to comfort her. She buried her face on his neck as she patted his huge, soft nose.

The brothers looked at each other, searching for the proper final words. Joseph casually lit his pipe. "I think this trip we're about to begin is more important to humanity than our previous one." He tried to smile. "This is a mission to save lives and guide humanity to a better course." He puffed unusually hard on his pipe. "The hardest part of this mission is saying goodbye," he added, on choked words. He turned his attention to the waiting canoe. He couldn't look at Gus any longer as his eyes were welling with tears.

Rubin nodded his head approvingly at his brother's words of wisdom. "Besides, this time we know the way and we know the people," he said with a nod.

As Gus stood looking at Rubin, he realized his younger brother had grown into a fine mature man, a man Gus was proud to call his brother. He knew he would miss Rubin most of all.

Gus grabbed him impulsively and hugged him. "Do take care of yourself, and him, as well," he said referring to Joe. He slapped Rubin on the shoulder and nodded his approval.

Rubin was taken unaware by his brother's emotional outburst but quickly said. "Of course, I'll take care." With a big smile and a nod toward Rachel, he added, "You take care of yourself and her too. She's the only sister-in-law I got, and you've got some work to do if Joe and I are going to be uncles." He returned the shoulder slap.

Their canoe, laden with supplies, was at the river's edge next to them. With a grin, Rubin continued, "Seems like big ole canoes and long trips on rivers is all our lives have been about these past few years."

That was the light moment they were looking for. Now it was time to shove off and begin yet one more epic trip.

After the somewhat emotional departure, Joseph and Rubin made just a few strokes with their canoe paddles before they stopped to look over their shoulders. They saw Gus standing with his hand held high waving. Rachel was standing by his side. She had composed herself and returned to bid them farewell. She too waved.

Their canoe was unique, inspired by the craft used on the Lewis and Clark Expedition. They expected to carry lots of supplies so they designed the craft to accommodate everything they wanted for comfort.

They quickly learned they had over done it.

On their previous trip into the unknown wilds, they nearly starved and froze to death several times. Sleeping in comfort on that expedition was just not possible. In fear of repeating their misery, they brought gear on this trip they could easily have done without.

They believed this excursion could take longer than the trip with Lewis and Clark. That would be more than two and a half years. The complexities of this message would require more time and effort to effectively communicate. Time and distance didn't matter as long as they were comfortable.

Comfort would create a positive attitude, they believed, and that positive attitude would allow for better communication. And better communication was essential for the success of this mission.

Their canoe was extra-long, extra wide, and, of course, extra heavy. It was tested several times and found to be river worthy. After many days on the river confessions were made that they should have tested it with a thousand pounds of something in it instead of only themselves. Now they had second thoughts. Landing and launching was troublesome too; they just had too much gear for one canoe.

They teased each other by recalling proverbs their mother had told them seemingly thousands of times over. "Don't put all your eggs in one basket," was a favorite.

Rubin would lovingly mock his mother, complete with body language and tone. Joseph laughed, but would never consider treading on the sacred ground of his mother's mannerisms. They both smiled warmly as they remembered her. "Don't put all your supplies in one canoe!" Rubin concluded sounding like his mom.

The extra width of the canoe made it more stable, but they still worried about capsizing. Had all their equipment been in one canoe on the Lewis and Clark trip, the adventure would have been over soon after it started. They had capsized one of those canoes, one carrying vital equipment. Some equipment was lost. More would have been lost if it wasn't for Sacajawea. The spirited young woman, quick of mind and action, saved many of the bundles of important equipment from the river.

Every time they mentioned her name they smiled and retold stories of her unlikely involvement with the expedition. The men of that epic trip spoke openly about her virtues.

Joe and Rubin unintentionally allowed themselves to be spiritually touched by events on the expedition. That acceptance of spirit, lead them to believe they had literally been selected by *God* to witness and learn from that journey.

And that is why Sacajawea was delivered to them. Her participation was absolutely essential. Not just any woman, but that particular woman.

She found natural medicines, gave priceless information on how to survive under any and all circumstances, and issued reassuring words of encouragement whenever needed.

The men all agreed during one of their post-trip debriefings that she had been sent to them by *God* to insure their survival and to show them their proper place in the world. They declared without hesitation that the success of their mission was totally to her credit.

One of the more extraordinary events of the Lewis and Clark expedition happened when they were desperately in need of food, horses and directions. They were hopelessly lost and starving. It was Sacajawea who found a wondering band of Indians to help. Out of thousands of miles of land that could have held bad mannered Indians, she found her long lost brother, now a tribal Chief. The mission was saved once again by *Devine* intervention. All their needs were provided for. Food, horses for over land traveling, and a guide. It was another example of *providence*. Their spiritual awakening was taking place. Soon thereafter, most of the team members would take time each day to humbly kneel and give thanks for their many blessings.

Only sixteen years old, she saved them from shame and ruin many times. Dedicated to the crew, her husband, and ultimately, her baby, she was never rewarded. She came from obscurity and after the expedition ended, sank back into obscurity.

The new canoe allowed better comfort while carrying more supplies. But, with just the one canoe, even with its extra width, the brothers remained cautious. Too much distance separated the front from the rear, making for poor communication. And shouting wasn't safe. Anyone in the area could hear, including pirates and hostile Indians.

Still, on more than one occasion, they remarked to each other that if they had to do it all over again, they would take two regular canoes instead of just one.

They both waved and watched till the canoe was out of sight. Gus felt exuberant but, just as the canoe faded out of sight, his emotions hit him. He was lonely now. His brothers, who were everything to him, had left him behind . . . again.

Joe told Gus, soon after their decision to make another journey that he would not be coming on this trip either.

Joe was right and Gus did not argue. Yet, deep down inside, he wondered about the adventures he was missing, while unknown to Gus, Joe wondered about the adventure of family life he was missing.

Gus trembled; Rachel hugged him and said, "They'll be all right. They've done this before." They both laughed as they walked back to their waiting surrey, wiping away their tears. Their future was waiting for them.

Rachel became excited and animated when she spoke of their future. They would all be living close to each other someday. Joe and Rubin would be married. Her dream included several nieces and nephews. It went without saying that she would also have a few sister-in laws too.

With Joseph and Rubin away on this new mission, she and Gus would farm the land and raise their children, crops and livestock. They will start to develop the land as they waited for Joe and Rubin to return and join with them as family, and as neighbors.

The settlement of the land grants owed to Joseph and Rubin proved interesting. They had been granted an existing homestead located in a place where white Americans were prohibited. All the land west of the Mississippi River was known as Indian Territory.

According to the new treaties made after the Louisiana Purchase, there were to be no settlers in the newly purchased territory. However, a French family had settled on the land when it was French territory. They had made peace with the Indians and lived beside them for decades before their land was sold to the new American government.

After the purchase, the French settlers were sent back to France. The Field brothers desired that one homestead. The final settlement skirted the edge of legality. But so did the Louisiana Purchase.

A tall and very thin land agent with plastered greasy hair provided words of caution before closing the deal. "You know you will be in Indian Territory and beyond the reach of help from American sources of any kind?"

"We know what we're getting into, sir," Gus replied.

"Do you really, now?" the land agent said contemptuously. "The French and the Indians have lived together in peace for generations out there because they are very much alike, savage heathens," he concluded.

Gus knew better than to argue, Rachel had her hand on his arm trying to keep him calm. Yet the reference to "savage heathens" had him steaming.

The land agent went on. "Those savages believe we white civilized Christians just go about shooting and cheating Indians for no good reason."

Gus jumped to his feet, reached over the table and pulled the skinny man up out of his chair by his lapels. "Now you listen to me, you lowlife weasel. My brothers have gone back into that land to tell the Indians what is really going to happen to them by civilized mad dogs like you. If it weren't for people like you in official positions, there wouldn't be a need for them to go anywhere but home where they belong. Gus pushed the skinny man back so hard he fell over his chair and hit the floor.

Gus had to admit, the skinny little man had spunk. The agent got back to his feet, still chattering away as if nothing had happened. "You say your brothers have gone back? Well, good riddance to them.

We decent Americans don't need to buy anything nor make a treaty with anyone. We can just take what we want." Now he was actually in Gus's face.

"You and your brothers are all insane!" He rapidly signed the deeds and procurement documents, then pushed them across the table at Gus. "Be on your way, you won't last long. The Indians will have your scalps hanging in their tents soon enough. From what I've heard they might even eat you. I hope they gag."

Gus slugged the little weasel so fast and hard he didn't even know he did it. With wide eyes, he looked first at the crumbled, unconscious heap of land agent on the floor, then to Rachel, sitting with her hands held to her mouth.

"Did I do that?" he asked, astonished.

"Yes, you did, and it was about time!" she replied with amusement.

They left the office with their documents in Rachel's shoulder bag, leaving the agent piled on the floor.

With agreements made and documents signed, they wished friends and family well. Rachel's father had come from Baton Rouge with one of her brothers just in time to say farewell. Promising to stay in touch, they planned to live on their land very soon.

Supplies and schedules were being readied. Gus and Rachel would soon be on their own journey, going home to a place they'd never been before.

CHAPTER SEVEN

Channeling their emotional energy into powerful strokes, Joseph and Rubin paddled their canoe effortlessly up the Missouri River for many miles before slowing their progress. Now their strong strokes exhausted them as they plied their canoe paddles. Their departure without Gus left them emotionally shocked and drained.

Joe stopped paddling and sat motionless in the front of the canoe watching the slow passage of the monotonous shoreline. He perspired heavily, out of breath from the exertion. Looking up the river, he felt like a barge on a sand bar, mired in a melancholy trap. For a moment he didn't know why he was there or what he was doing. He knew only that one of his brothers wasn't with him, and that made him feel as though he couldn't breathe properly.

Rubin cleared his throat loudly trying to get Joe's attention, it went unnoticed. He tried a second time much louder. Joe heard it and snapped out of his reverie. He responded with a stunned look at Rubin. Sitting in the rear of the canoe, Rubin was trying hard to break the spell Joe had fallen under.

Rubin spoke louder than he should have. "Remember you said you were proud to be a torch carrier, remember you said that this time we're exploring to find a better path for all of mankind?" He grinned broadly, even though the smile was manufactured. He had broken the rule of being too loud but thought it necessary, even critical, to do so.

Joe half-turned in his seat, focusing on Rubin. He thought he saw dried tear tracks on his face. Joe studied him for a long moment. He wanted to tell him how proud and honored he was to have him for a brother and exploring companion. He wanted to tell him how much he loved him and that he thought he was a great brother. But he remained quiet, unsure of expressing himself in such a way. He squandered an opportunity.

Rubin was struggling with his own issues over his brothers. He wanted to laugh it off but couldn't. He saw both his brothers in pain and couldn't comfort them. He too wondered why he was here.

The smile on Joe's face was nearly unnoticeable under his shaggy beard; Rubin could see the smile in his eyes though. That made him feel better, putting a shine in his smile that had been, until now, missing.

"Gus and Rachel will be all right, and so will we," Joe said with reassuring authority. Then he fell into deep thought again and let a little time pass before he added with genuine astonishment, "And think of it, Rubin: We will have family and land of our own to come back to. Life will be good then."

Rubin surprised Joe with his reply. "But first we need to warn the Indians that things will be different from what we said the first time we visited. Let's hope it will all work out." After a few moments of reflection, he added, "Then maybe we can live in peace with all our fellow countrymen, white people and Indians."

Joe nodded his acceptance of Rubin's statement and conceded to himself that his youngest brother had in fact developed into a deep, mature man.

"Well said," Joe replied with a wink. He then turned forward again and the brothers continued paddling their canoe up the Missouri River.

The trip into the land of the Lakota Indians, via the Missouri River, was virtually trouble free. Joseph and Rubin had few problems managing their provision-laden canoe.

The experience from their previous expedition with the Lewis-Clark team had given them the confidence needed to undertake a mission such as this on their own. They were less apprehensive than before. They handled the oversized and overloaded canoe with the expertise of masters of the river and well-experienced canoeists.

The winter they had just spent in St. Louis had been better because they had been at home. The previous winter had been spent in mountains that would become known as the Rocky Mountains. That stay had been miserable and life-threatening. They never wanted to go back there.

Eight months had passed since they had completed the expedition with the Lewis and Clark team. They had returned from that expedition along this same watery highway. Thus far it seemed as though little had changed since then. Fear of the dangers waiting around the next bend did not exist on this trip. The nervous apprehension that had ignited their adrenaline drives was now replaced by an energy that kindled confidence and determination.

"This is the way it should be done," Joseph would say from time to time.

"And this is the way it should feel," Rubin replied.

No more did they labor at mapping, collecting and surveying. Nor did either man miss any of the tedious camp chores that had seemed as endless as the river. Lewis and Clark were military men and they ran the mission in a military way. Clean orderly camp sites, guard duty, and scouting patrols were all missing from this journey.

The chronicles of the trip as it had occurred day by day, as well as specimens collected and catalogued, had been sent by expedition courier back along the river. The brothers now traveled without spending time compiling tedious notes and charts then sending them onto Washington.

The personal attention given to those duties came from Meriwether Lewis. He had been President Thomas Jefferson's personal secretary and friend for many years. Then he had been placed in a unique position on the expedition. His life, the life of Captain Clark, and the lives of countless other people had been changed forever.

The first five weeks passed quickly. It was now the end of June. Spring floods supplied them with enough challenges to keep them busy. Traveling upstream was hard enough, but the extra flow and drifting debris tested their skills. Soon though, the river would settle down as the snow melt ended. The brothers were happy to have covered as much ground in five weeks as the expedition had in three months.

Their encounters with Indians they met along the way were beginning to take up just little bit too much time they thought. From the beginning of their journey they expected to stay a night or two with any transient scouting party they may encounter or tribe that was hospitable and could be reasonably communicated with. They wanted to take enough time to explain the reason for their trip without spending too much time in one place with one group. They conveyed to the natives that it was essential for them to pass their message along to any and all tribes possible.

Much to their surprise they were getting enthusiastic cooperation from the Indians. They seemed to be very eager to help. Joseph and Rubin had taken extra precautions to make certain they were properly understood. They didn't want wrong or inaccurate words to be expressed to anyone. The message they conveyed to the natives while on the Lewis and Clark expedition had changed. The message they now brought was sincere and true.

The fledgling government of America found treaties easy to make, and break. The rules and plans were only a general guide. The system was made so consideration for constant change would always be accepted. Business people with lawyers found amendments easily affordable. Many years later, people of integrity and honor would hang their heads in shame and disgust over the government's handling of Indian affairs.

Feasting and smoking were a part of every tribal visit, and it wore the brothers down. How much lean meat could a man's system take before digestive problems started to occur? And every tribe had its own version of beverages and smokes. That, too, took its toll, though more on Rubin than Joe.

Indians always expected gifts to be exchanged with any passerby and the Field brothers did not disappoint them. They knew the Indians had a love for tobacco, so the brothers had procured a large supply of the best tobacco they could find, along with an equally large supply of pipes to be given away as often as needed as tokens of friendship.

Interesting legends and lore accepted about Native Americans would in later years be scrutinized and found to be void of merit. As an example, some people, who knew nothing factual about the real Native Americans, said they loved to smoke tree bark and grasses. During the expedition, the brothers had dispelled that ridiculous myth. Instead of tree bark or grass, they did however have many different mixes of carefully cultured tobaccos. They understood the agricultural aspect of this popular commodity.

They traded tobacco and other smoking items freely among other tribes, starting long before the arrival of the white man. The pipes they used ranged from very basic to pieces of magnificent art.

Visiting with tribes living along the river, or close to it, gave Joe and Rubin good reason to believe their goodwill and message would precede them upriver and over the land. The brothers didn't know how far they would have to travel or with whom they might have to speak to. They only knew they had to make the urgency of their message understood. With faith and confidence they proceeded up the Missouri River, their final destination unknown.

CHAPTER EIGHT

Rubin and Joseph had only been gone a few weeks before things started coming together for Gus and Rachel. The date of departure to their homestead rapidly approached. Deeds had been signed; provisions crated and loaded final good-byes and gratitude shown. Last and very important, was a solemn visit to the cemetery where Viola Field had been laid to rest. Now Gus and Rachel were ready to start their adventure. Readied crews, and nervous animals, were all staged to travel into the Louisiana Territory to the junction of the Platte, Elkhorn, and Missouri Rivers. They were going home.

The Louisiana Territory was purchased in 1803 by President Thomas Jefferson. Purchase price was fifteen million dollars. That money bought forty-five million acres, give or take a few hundred acres. The controversial decision had been made by a visionary president to double the size of the United States for about thirty cents an acre. Gus and Rachel's land, combined with Joe and Rubin's, lay in an area that would in 1821 be called Nebraska. But for now it was a lonely homestead in Indian Territory. The deal was negotiated, site unseen.

Gus and Rachel's journey took them by prairie schooner from St. Louis almost four hundred miles northwest, traveling alongside the Missouri River.

Their settlement, they were told, lay within eyesight of the Platte River, a waterway the Oto Indians called "Nebrathka," meaning "flat water.

They hired a professional cattle driving crew to drive one hundred and fifty head of cattle to their homestead. This was a short cattle drive compared to most. Gus had been told these men were experienced and could handle anything happening on the journey. He and Rachel hadn't expected politeness and courtesy to come out of these hard looking men. They seemed to be very competent and knowledgeable. Gus and Rachel were gratified to be accompanied by these men.

The move from St. Louis to their homestead took a long miserable six weeks. Moving in springtime was not their first choice but, as crews of people and herds of animals came together, they had to go when everything was ready.

Another crew of hired men handled the horses and cared for all the other animals being transported for use on the farm. Hogs and hens were crated, loaded and traveled on covered wagons. The goats Rachel loved so much were allowed to follow at their own will. They did so much to her relief, but to insure they stay close they tethered the lead goat to the wagon. The rest would instinctively follow her.

Four stubborn oxen slowly pulled their schooner. Another schooner was driven by a hired man and his wife. These schooners were loaded with enough household items for them to set up a comfortable home. Despite padding, the violent shaking and constant movement made riding on the bench intolerable. Gus and Rachel chose to walk and lead their teams of oxen as much as they could.

Gus compared the ox to some of the men he had seen in St. Louis spending their money recklessly and behaving irresponsibly. The oxen were hairy, much like the raw crude men working on some of the river barges. Their bodies stank, as did the men, and they flatulated more than any animal had a right to, just like the men. And not one of the oxen was cooperative. Gus lost his patience with one of the animals and decided to shoot it simply because of its disposition, but Rachel scornfully prohibited it. "You have to be more patient with them," she told him. "You just don't know how to handle these adorable creatures." She got more cooperation from them by scratching their chins and talking to them like they were small children. They followed her like puppies.

The government provided a stock of high grade cattle as part of Rubin and Joseph's settlement from the expedition. These animals were vital to the existence of any homesteader. Cattle had many uses if managed properly. They were a source of meat and trade goods. Their hides served as clothing material. Strips of sinew were cut thin and dried, then used for tying and binding. Other parts of the hide were used for shoes and boots. The bones could be used for many types of tools and weapons.

Gus was relieved to find the herd was being watched over very well by the men he hired. He eventually gave in to Rachel's insistence that he relax and enjoy the trip. Anticipated problems from wolves, pumas, and storms never materialized. Any of these things could have scattered the herd in an instant. The hired team leader impressed Gus with his knowledge, maturity, and his determination to do things efficiently and safely while giving Gus and Rachel just enough room to have a bit of privacy. He debated Gus about keeping the herd farther away in case there was trouble. Gus wanted them closer. He conceded and the foreman set up the teams and drove the herd without a single incidence. The foreman's obvious expertise was the main reason Gus could relax. It was hard for him to depend on men other than his brothers for help. But he was learning how to.

Still Gus remained vigilant, constantly watching over the entire group of people and animals. He kept his rifle close and loaded at all times. They had been nearly a week on the trail before he could relax. The rifle now rode under the schooners bench.

Anticipation about traveling with Rachel proved to be pointless also. He was more concerned about her comfort and safety in the beginning of the trip than he was now. She impressed and surprised him by never complaining. In fact she seemed to handle the hardships of the trip better than he did. Many times, as he was walking along trying to lead the oxen (and having very little success) she would walk up to them, talk gently to them, and actually get the stubborn beast to cooperate. He noticed her innocent little girl way of picking flowers as they walked along. She would skip over to the oxen and hold the flowers under their noses as if she wanted to share the bouquet with them. Gus thought he witnessed an ox sniff, and then nod its approval. He knew then more than ever just how lucky he was to have her in his life. She made the rough, hard job of moving all these animals and people safely over the land a pleasant journey.

One afternoon, while slowly following the heard and the drivers, (ahead of them by almost a mile) she urgently asked him to stop. Amazingly the oxen stood still and became quiet when she hushed them. Gus immediately felt concerned about Indians. He retrieved his rifle from under the schooner bench. She said softly she thought she heard someone cry out for help.

He listened intently. Rachel had her ear turned toward the faint noise. They both jerked simultaneously, silently confirming they had indeed heard a man screaming for help. With rifle in hand, Gus raced along in the general direction of the wailing plea, searching for its source.

The sight he beheld would have been amusing, had it not been for the obvious danger the person was in. A muscular looking black man clung near the top of a slender tree, crying out for help. The tree was bending over under the strain of this refugee, barely keeping the man out of reach of four snarling, snapping wolves.

Gus realized he had to do something quick. He didn't want to shoot and draw attention to themselves and this black man. He rapidly weighed his options knowing white men could be more dangerous to a black man than wolves. He picked up a long stick and raised it and his rifle in his hands. He spread his arms and tried to look bigger than he was. Then he rushed the wolves as he screamed. He didn't want to kill them unless he had to; yet it took all his courage to stand against them. He remembered having been told many times, "show no fear with animals, look them straight in the eyes and approach them defiantly." It did the trick. The wolves ran away. The frightened black man climbed down out of the tree. Gus was winded from the sprint and confrontation. But even now he could barely suppress his laughter.

"I's be much thankful sur," he panted, dripping wet from perspiration. He wrung his worn out hat in his hands. "I's be prayin and then there you was." His dark eyes looked up towards the heavens when he thanked God for his deliverance, once again revealing the whites in his eyes. Gus could barely contain his urge to laugh out loud.

Gus and Rachel gave the overly excited man a drink of water and listened to his story. His name was Rainier and he was a runaway slave from Mississippi. Being a runaway slave was a very serious matter. Abolitionist and other people who would assist a runaway slave could be, and often were hung. The runaway would then be beaten, humiliated, then returned to the proper owner. A bounty would be paid to the captor. The pitiful human would then resume the life of a slave, only they would have to wear shackles around their ankles, maybe for the rest of their life.

Gus and Rachel had never believed in the philosophy of slavery. The only person Gus had ever known to own a slave was Captain William Clark. That was a troubling aspect about the expedition. The Field brothers tried to overlook the problem, and even tried to understand it with the help of Captain Clark's explanation. But it never made sense and always made them feel just a little less respectful of Captain Clark. Though York was treated as an equally free man on the expedition, and even though he acted like a free man, he was still the personal property of William Clark. He was denied basic human rights and was considered by slave owners and others who believed in slavery as little more than livestock. Yet to all the men of the expedition, York was just one of the men, well liked and respected.

Gus and Rachel offered Rainier food and water and encouraged him to keep running. But Rainier convinced them they could use a good hand on their homestead and made them a deal that was acceptable to all. He proposed that he could work for a room to sleep in and have meals provided. Gus added in the deal that he would always have the right to refuse work and be able to leave whenever he wanted. Rainier was surprised when Gus held out his hand to shake. "We shake hands on it and it seals the deal," Gus said.

Rainier shook hands with Gus and said, "*God* bless you and the Mrs., Sur."

It took another three days struggling with the schooner before they arrived at their homestead. They kept Rainier out of sight during those last few days of travel. They didn't want to take any chances with any of the hired crew. If any of them saw Rainier and believed in slavery, everyone's dreams would end.

Rainier agreed to lay low and stay quiet in the schooner, waiting till the hired men had been paid, thanked and dismissed.

After Gus and Rachel had evaluated their homestead, and the land of Rubin and Joe's, they were glad they accepted Rainier's proposition. They considered him a *God* send.

The homestead had become infested with varmints. Evicting such residents became an immediate priority. Other than that, the farm house was in remarkable condition, they all fell humbly to their knees and gave a prayer of thanks.

There were a few stumps remaining from the trees that were cut to provide lumber to build the house. One of them was huge. It would require a lot of hard work to remove. Gus declared the homestead as a work in progress noting that it would remain so for the foreseeable future.

The stones for the chimney, fireplace, and foundation were obviously mined from the nearby river. With everything else, serious cleaning still remained before moving into the house was possible.

Several months had past since Joseph and Rubin departed on their spiritually inspired journey. There had been no word from them on their whereabouts or on their condition so far. Gus was beginning to get concerned. It was a major effort for him to act as if nothing out of the ordinary was going on. He didn't want to trouble Rachel with unfounded worries.

Yet Rachel had begun worrying as well. She tried hard not to let Gus know just how concerned she had become about his brothers. So they each played their own little game of trying to not let the other know how worried they were, even though they both harbored the same apprehensions.

This was, however, part of frontiers people's lives. They could not allow themselves to become too concerned about anyone who had gone exploring or homesteading. It was all too common not to hear anything from such people for many months or even years. They heard of folks who had gone out to homestead and were never heard from again. Faith was all they had to carry themselves through till the day would come when some news would find them. Keeping busy was the way to avoid thinking too much about the people they loved and missed. Their homestead certainly kept their minds and bodies busy.

The view from the rise where their home stood was breath taking. Gus stood on the porch in the frosty early morning light warming himself with a third cup of coffee. He looked out over the valley he could now call his own. He gave quiet, reverent thanks for this blessing. Their herd of cattle grazed along both sides of the narrow river that cut through the valley in both directions.

A small village of Indians could be seen far to the east on the property. There were two lodges and three tipis. The land agent told Gus before they left St. Louis, that a small band of destitute, mixed tribe of people dwelled on his property. The agent also said he should have no problem removing them. Gus was troubled by the way the agent said "remove."

Mixed tribes people? He had observed the little village through a telescope, wondering if they watched him also. Many Indians had small field scopes they received as gifts from explorers and traders, so it wasn't unreasonable to expect them to be watching him. A visit to the village would soon be in order.

The Indian lodges appeared to be earthen mounds, with some stones and roughhewn timbers in the construction. Pawnees were known for building this kind of home. Were they peaceful? Gus surmised if they were not, he would have known it by now.

CHAPTER NINE

The Bostonian fire and brimstone preacher, Father Ross, always looked sternly down on his congregation. Some people said he had been born with a fierce expression, others said he was simply possessed. And there were those who believed he had been taught to look that way by the Catholic priest who raised him. He was left on the doorstep of a church as a five-month-old. Some said his mother saw or felt something about her child she felt only a priest could correct or placate. Whatever the reason, no matter his age, he had always acted in a mean and vindictive manner. He had no girlfriend in his youth, and very few male friends. In his mature years, he still had no woman to love and call his own. Sexual frustration caused him to vilify women.

Andrew Bartholomew Ross was a man who found his only comfort in the words of the Bible. Common people didn't measure up to his standards and, unfortunately, common people were almost all that entered his life. He had grown up to become a priest who frightened his congregation with his tirades over social and personal ills. His congregation followed and obeyed him not out of love or respect, but out of fear . . . the fear of eternal damnation. Father Ross had defined and implanted that caustic revelation in their minds.

Good Christians and other decent people avoided Father Ross. They knew Christian love and fellowship forbade the bigoted behavior he preached. They rejected his rhetoric. Good Christians directed their attention to a different mission, dedicating themselves to preaching love, tolerance, and peaceful living among all people on earth, remaining steadfast for centuries. However, there has always been and will always be a small measure of bad clergymen. These imposters of righteousness and violators of sacred orders, such as Father Ross, always found their own special group of followers. Those who followed the likes of Ross posed a danger to the fundamentals of basic good human behavior.

Father Ross hated Indians. He considered them sub-human. He loathed the poor and blacks as well. He liked the Chinese because they were subservient. They rarely made eye contact and executed orders rapidly without question.

Father Ross felt disgust for those who failed to be, by his standards, better Christians. He expected everyone to strive toward becoming a better Christian in some way — in particular, his way. Those who rejected, or remained ambivalent about the message of the Bible, invoked in him a murderous rage. A domineering Catholic priest from the eastern United States, he too, realized his mission early in his career: taking the message of salvation and redemption to the unbelievers. He alleged *God* called upon him to take the word of salvation to the uninitiated. He believed his naturally strong system of converting non- believers as a gift.

But it was his interpretation of the Bible he wanted them to learn. He thought if more people were like him the world would be a better place for all. And he would convert them, or destroy them in the process, for their own salvation he would say. Blasphemy and sacrilege, according to Father Ross's dark and unforgiving mind, called for immediate death. He knew the clergy controlled the law and the land a few centuries ago in Europe. He wanted the clergy to be the law of the land of The United States as well. And death for those who felt differently, he believed, should be slow and torturous, just as it was centuries ago. He smiled whenever he thought of perverted torture. He couldn't help himself.

The message from the informant in St. Louis alerted Father Ross to the existence of the Wooesa. He gleaned from the message that these Indians were able to communicate directly with *God*. Just the thought enraged him. Consulting with missionaries who had visited the Indians of the western frontier, Father Ross learned *The Wooesa* were known as *"The Real People."* The missionaries and the Indians believed this special tribe lived as *Wankan Tonka, The Great Spirit*, intended, and that these people had done much to bridge the gap between white people and Indians.

Hearing this was more than the priest could handle. A shrill cry spewed from the maddened priest's mouth. "Sacrilege!" he wailed. "I shall be the one who saves lost souls, not heathens living like animals." He struggled with himself to maintain some sort of self-control. His quiet, dark, church served as the only witness to his delusional rant.

If anyone had been close to the church and was listening, they would have heard Father Ross screaming through his frothing lips. "Those sacrilegious blasphemers must die for this sin!" He had worked himself up into an intoxicated sense of self-righteousness.

Pacing the floor of the church alone, he visualized the threat these savages posed to weak-minded frontiersmen and women. "Those poor fools might listen to those savages," he shouted out loud. His slipping sanity was scheming merciless deeds of madness.

He heard of settlers befriending Indians and he didn't approve. He preached to his congregation that such actions would cast the soul of a person into eternal damnation. In his most recent sermons he had said, "The only way to insure a white person keeps his soul from misdirection by the savages is to kill those who refuse to accept the word," he patted the Bible, and then added venomously, "Especially the ones calling themselves *The Wooesa.*"

An assembly of zealous fanatics was easy to recruit. A few words from Father Ross about the wrath of *God* guaranteed a company of crusaders would volunteer.

The followers of Ross believed their deeds and doctrines were designed to keep the people of the frontier from losing their souls to pagan ideologies. With the country barely thirty years old, everyone had either been a frontiersman or knew someone who was. Everyone knew about the problems isolation from civilization caused. White men of several cultures married Indian women with regularity.

The opinion of many American citizens, propagated through the media and the clergy of some churches, implied that the citizens were not only entitled to the entire continent, but were obligated to take it by any means.

Settling the land west of the Mississippi as quickly as humanly possible became the unofficial goal. No one talked about the race they were in with other nations, but the competition to claim the land spawned companies of zealous, murderous crusaders.

It was genocide to the Indian nation. Invaders were coming from different countries. Help was not coming. Resistance would be futile. Yet this madness was the will of *Wankan Tanka*.

Adding to the problems of the Indians were rumors that gold waited to be panned, mined, or just found sitting on top of the ground. Other unbelievable rumors created a toxic formula that caused eyes of same men to glaze over. Whole communities began to organize westward treks to claim free land. If they encountered Indians, they expected to simply kill them, thereby making the country safe for civilized white people. Father Andrew Bartholomew Ross intended to lead one such crusade along the path the Lewis and Clark team had taken. His theory was that they would be well received because of the good will that preceded them.

He was convinced it was his destiny to venture into the frontier and save souls from damnation. He now sat on his butt on the hard floor, rocking back and forth, holding himself tightly, his eyes rolled up in his head. He began muttering unintelligible words, his form of personal prayer to his *God*.

CHAPTER TEN

Soft, pre-dawn light illuminated the valley as Gus stepped out of the house and onto the front porch. The brisk morning air had a refreshing, wake up effect, giving him reason to smile. The wooden porch beneath his feet softly creaked in mock protest to his slow, heavy footsteps. Inhaling a deep breath, he stopped to lean against a post supporting the roof over the porch.

The valley came into sharper view as the sun rose. The sight moved him spiritually, as it always did. This was his favorite time of day. Looking up into the morning sky, he saw it still held a few stars, remaining there as though they were waiting for him to say good night before they disappeared.

"Thank you, *God*," he whispered softly. "Thank you for all of this." He closed his eyes for a moment of quiet meditation. The morning mist rose above the water of the nearby Platte River. The ghostly image, flowing slowly toward heaven, added a reverent effect to the morning view. Gus felt as though *God* had granted him this special moment so they could commune together. Once again he whispered with reverence, "Thank you."

To the far east of their property, smoke wisped from the round holes in the roofs of the Indian lodges in the village at the river's edge, like white threads rising up into the sky. Gus had been told these people were a mixed group of Arapaho and Pawnee, two tribes historically known as peaceful farmers. They settled on a high bank close to the water's edge, obviously to stay dry and safe. An intelligent move, Gus thought.

The river was a highway and the Indians were well located to conduct trade with whoever traveled upon it. Obviously not hostile — there had been no threats or trouble — it was evident from the gardens the Indians maintained they intended to stay and survive.

The land agent told Gus the savages would be little or no problem to remove. The greasy, overly-perfumed, thin man gave a noticeable wink and a nod, an unspoken invitation to do whatever he wanted to do with the Indians. Gus remembered the contemptuous weasel and the disrespect he showed for the natives of the land.

A philosophical paradox presented itself to Gus. He and his brothers believed all the land belonged to the Indians with all their varied tribes and clans. And now they found themselves claiming ownership of land they knew at one time belonged to the Indians.

For decades it had been owned by French settlers who had been bought out as part of the Louisiana Purchase. The Indians hadn't laid claim to the property in all that time. There were no pending ownership discrepancies. Knowledge of what must have been decades or centuries ago, and what now is by some *Higher Design*, had to pacify him.

Treaties were written and stated the land belonged to the Indians and would not be taken by white settlers. But despite reassurances about sanctity of word and deed, a technically advanced culture found wealth easy to take from a culture still using flint pointed arrows, slings and lances.

Gus thought about the complexities of land ownership in the case of the Indians. They had been here since the beginning and claimed this land belonged to everyone, no deed needed.

Spanish, French, Russian and probably a few other unknown countries saw an opportunity to acquire and control the resources of this continent.

The Indians were in trouble of losing their land to invading nations. Downfall of their culture was inevitable.

The Americans had a better foot hold on the continent. They were established and growing stronger every year. Industries had monopolies and financially controlled policy makers. Lawyers acting legally obtained as much as possible for their clients and themselves. It was too easy for the white culture to seize control of the land.

Gus knew little about land deals outside of his own. But he was urged by lawyers to find land while they were legally beyond the boundaries of others. "A unique opportunity to make a fortune with no competition," a lawyer said. He was told he could make a thousand percent on his money in a short amount of time. He and his brothers would never consider doing such a deal. But they thought of how many others would. His brothers, as well as other people of decent character, agreed.

Certain government agencies implicated their part in the conspiracy to defraud the Indians. They did this by declaring it illegal to sell the same land back to them. Those laws wouldn't change for decades. The Indian Chiefs, who knew the value of their land and tried to make a better bargain for them, were dealt with in a more deadly manor.

The white culture, including the French, Spanish, Russians, and British, planned to expand the size of their holdings by swindles and deadly seizures, also. The Indians had one plan until the insurgence of white Europeans, live and let live. *Wankan Tonka* allowed them to count coup, but outright wars between Indian tribes were more infrequent than believed.

It proved easy to take advantage of the Indians. And most people thought it unnecessary to compromise with *"the savages"* in any way at all. Settlers were encouraged to take whatever they wanted or needed by force, and keep whatever they could by force. This was the unwritten law of the land east of the Mississippi. The Field brothers knew it would also be the law of the land west of the Mississippi. And they knew it would happen soon, very soon.

Gus and Rainier kept a sharp eye on the little village, thinking they would be visited soon. They had on many occasions noticed the Indians standing still and looking their way. Gus continued to wonder if maybe someone in that little village had a small telescope. Curiosity began to get the best of him and he knew he would have to pay them a visit very soon. But, for now, all was peaceful and that was good enough. Besides, he thought it would be best to train Rainier to assist him and not go alone.

Gus struck a match to light the cigarette he had just rolled. He inhaled deeply. Rachel walked out of the house and joined him. The porch boards gave not a single squeak, no protest at all to her soft, light, feminine steps. He straightened himself and turned to face her. She reached for him and tenderly wrapped her warm, loving arms around him. They stood wrapped together as one and became lost in each other's tender, loving embrace.

Turning their faces toward the valley they sighed with inner contentment and relief. They knew they had finally arrived. They were home.

This was a special time in their lives and they knew good things would come from their efforts to live in peace.

Gus felt her warmth and softness within his embrace. His arms were large, muscular, and hairy. They became a protective shroud around her, pulling her close. Squeezing her tenderly, he looked into her eyes and smiled.

"You make me so happy." He kissed her forehead. She pressed her face into his chest. "But I got lots of work to do today," he said in a whisper, kindly trying to dismiss her.

She turned in his arms. He held her from behind. She pulled his arms up under her bosom and ran her fingers through the course hair of his arms. "I felt our baby move this morning," she said softly, almost dreamily.

He hugged her tenderly, yet firmly, enveloping her with love and protection.

She was seven months along in her pregnancy and her size was beginning to impede her every movement. She felt as happy as she could be, with a new home, a loving man, and a child on the way.

This is what they had planned for and patiently waited on since moving from St. Louis. It was now early August and they figured their child would arrive in late October or early November. Rachel re-entered the house after a gentle kiss. Gus, beaming, stepped down from the porch.

He wondered about how he would handle child delivery. Before their departure from St. Louis, they both had been instructed by the local physician in the basic procedures of childbirth. Rachel packed several books on the subject, adding them to her small library of home medical procedures. She already had many opportunities to practice basic first aid on Gus and Rainier. The men would have normally ignored the cuts, abrasions, joint and muscle sprains and strains, but she was always insistent about nursing and doctoring them and the animals. She referred to the books often.

Yet, childbirth on the frontier was hazardous at best. They tried to prepare the best way they could. Gus had been rehearsing in his mind his roll when her labor started. The bigger she got, the more nervous he became.

He asked Rainier one day if he had any experience with women giving birth. He was becoming desperate for knowledge and needed more support and encouragement.

With a smile, Gus remembered Rainier's reply, "When da woman start to scream wif da child, I jus go to da barn and wait."

Gus had looked Rainier straight in the eye and said, "Good advice, Rainier." He was trying not to laugh. He then asked in mock seriousness knowing repair of the barn's roof was still in progress. "Is our barn ready for us to go to?"

"No, sir, but it will be when da child come," Rainier said with wide-eyed sincerity. Then he narrowed his eyes in concentration and added, "Ya know, sir, I suppose if you gotta help your wife wif da child to come out, you kin jus grab da baby by da arms and jus pull, kinda like what you does wif da cow or da horse."

Gus couldn't control himself this time and he let out a roar of laughter. "Do you suppose it will be that easy, Rainier?" Gus asked.

Rainier once again narrowed his eyes in deep concentration, then said, "You know, sir, the ways I got it figured, a woman be smaller dan da horse or cows so's I suppose it be easier."

Gus stared at Rainier with humored disbelief. Rainier's innocent, naive outlook on life was as much blessing to him as his strength and ability to work hard for long periods of time and never complaining.

He was endearing to Rachel and he had a natural talent for softening the hard issues of the day with his childlike charm and humor. Gus was deeply grateful for his assistance and company.

CHAPTER ELEVEN

Looking over his shoulder, Joseph called out to Rubin. "We should consider landing this boat and making camp for the night."

Rubin nodded his head in silent approval.

"It'll be dark before long and we should have a good meal and a long rest," Joe added. He was breathing laboriously.

Rubin noticed how tired his older brother had been acting lately. He wondered if maybe Joseph wasn't getting a little too old for this kind of adventure. He nodded again, acknowledging Joe's suggestion, and smiled with approval. The strenuous effort of paddling their canoe upstream, into the current, was hard on him too.

As they traveled, the river gorge kept narrowing. The narrower channel meant a stronger current. The effort to navigate waters such as these took all their strength, skill, and breath. Their muscles ached from the strain. A good meal and a long rest would be most welcome.

The suggestion to land the canoe had been rhetorical. They had come to the end of this navigable part of the river and were faced with a rock-filled gauntlet. A tumultuous stretch of white water lay before them.

The rapids cascaded over and down a narrow hill to empty into a large, almost perfectly round basin where they now floated. Another river, the

Cheyenne, merged with the Missouri at this point. They looked up at the rapids as the water splashed and rolled toward them.

Below the rapids lay a large pool with a continuous counterclockwise swirling movement. Foam defined the perimeter of the whirlpool. Words of warning were unnecessary. They both paddled as far away from the rapidly swirling foam as they possibly could.

"You're right, I'm starving, and I need to put my feet on solid ground." Rubin finally agreed out loud.

They carefully scanned the shore as they drifted closer, locating a spot that looked flat, grassy, and comfortable. Rubin used his paddle as a rudder to turn the canoe hard to one side. Satisfied all looked clear, they nodded to each other. They gave the canoe a few final, deep, powerful strokes to drive the canoe into the soft bank.

They immediately relaxed. "Let's call it a day," Rubin said with a yawn.

Joe stood up in the front of the canoe and stretched, looking around. "Nice place for a home," he said.

"It's our home for the night," Rubin responded.

It was a great campsite. The soft sandy loam and grasses made excellent bedding. Dry wood for a campfire was plentiful. These things, combined with the sibilant sounds of the rapids, made a naturally relaxing atmosphere. To top it all off, in only a few minutes they caught enough fish for both evening and morning meals.

They awakened with their strength restored. After breakfast, they packed all their gear and hiked with it along the riverbank to get around the unnavigable rapids. The river narrowed and turned into a raging stretch of water for about a mile. Stopping once to observe the power of the rapids, Rubin said with conviction.

"I wouldn't want to take our canoe through that." Joe agreed with a nod and a hard puff on his pipe. It took several trips back and forth before all their gear and the canoe were together again.

Rubin climbed in first and took his place in the rudder position.

Joe looked about checking to see if they had forgotten anything. Satisfied all was well he nodded, they were ready to launch. The canoe was stuck fast in the soft bank. They loaded it without moving it more into the water, another oversight giving them reason to laugh at themselves.

"Just put your back into it and shove like you mean it," Rubin said with his humorous tone.

Joseph gave out a loud grunt as he pushed.

"What ya trying to do, wake the dead?" Rubin asked with laughter in his voice.

A disturbed bear roared from a nearby thicket causing their heart beats to double.

Without delay, they struggled with the canoe, trying to free it from the bank. Rubin paddled frantically backward. Joseph pushed hard against the canoe. They remained stuck fast! They had to get the canoe out into the river NOW! The bear crashed out of the thicket just as the canoe came free from the bank.

"Jump in!" Rubin shouted hysterically.

The bear, running fast, rapidly closed the distance between them. Joseph dove into the canoe, pulling himself into fetal position just as the bear snapped its jaws closed barely missing his legs. Rubin paddled deep and rapidly, but the cumbersome canoe was moving too slow. The bear followed them out into the river, clawing and snapping at the canoe.

In a panic, Joseph grabbed the canoe paddle and struck the bear repeatedly on the head. They had been caught like two novice frontiersmen without their guns at the ready.

The canoe paddle had to be enough to repel the bear. Joseph couldn't take even a second to grab his rifle. Again and again he struck the bear over the head. As he kept up his defensive assault, the paddle split and splintered and was finally reduced to a long pointed dagger. Yet the bear raged relentlessly trying to capsize the boat to spill them into the water.

Joe kept up his battle, praying he could poke out one of the bear's eyes with the remains of his paddle. Still, the bear snapped at him with a vicious, frothing mouth filled with murderous, dagger-like teeth.

Joseph jabbed at the bear's head. The bear turned slightly and seized the paddle stub in its mouth pulling it from his hands. At last, it turned away and swam to shore.

"Looks like it's satisfied with your paddle," Rubin said with a trembling, panting voice. They watched the bear make its way to the bank and chew what was left of the paddle into small splinters.

"That was way too close!" Joe said, collapsing on his back in the canoe. "Let's make sure we don't make that mistake again," he said trembling and exhausted.

Rubin was still paddling the canoe out toward the deeper presumably safer part of the river, hoping to discourage further attacks by the bear once it devoured the paddle. He had yet to realize they had gone from one bad situation to another that was even worse. Now in the center of the river, they were in the strongest current. An ominous pull dragged them into the beginning of the rapids they hiked around.

Exhausted and unprepared for the power of the river's current, Rubin struggled to keep them from the rapids while Joseph frantically searched for their spare paddle.

They were drawn into the currents flow like metal to a magnet. Rubin was powerless to save them. His failing strength played an intricate part in the plan of their *destiny*. The bear, no paddle, misplaced drag line; all had a vital part in this plan.

Not able to locate a spare paddle, Joseph looked toward Rubin anxiously. "Where did we put our anchor and line?" he shouted nervously.

Rubin shook his head, too busy with a different battle. The situation was tense and near out of control. He fought bravely paddling the canoe, trying to get some kind of control.

Shouting at Rubin with a panic-stricken voice, Joe said, "Jump and swim!"

Rubin couldn't swim, so he never considered it. Instead of jumping, he clenched his teeth and began to stroke harder than before. He had to save his brother.

"Look far ahead and don't think, just react!" Joe told him on the expedition when Rubin had to paddle a canoe flawlessly or be dumped into an icy, raging flood-swollen stream. Now he recalled vividly every detail of the situation. The big difference then had been there were two men paddling the canoe. Now it was just himself, using the only paddle they could find, and this canoe responded more slowly than a regular canoe. And he was exhausted. Joseph had found the anchor, but was engaged in untangling the line.

Joe focused on a spot on the bank of the river, hoping it was far enough away from the bear's territory to allow them to put ashore. "There, over there," he shouted.

He was always optimistic and never gave up. That would be their destination if they could only beat the powerful current. Rubin tried hard to control the canoe, yet his labor was in vain. The river's current was too strong. They rapidly approached a splashing, wet, pounding, icy cold, death, and there appeared nothing to keep them from it. Rubin was so exhausted he could barely hold onto his paddle.

CHAPTER TWELVE

"What a spectacular view!" Rubin quipped nervously. It was a perspective he wished he didn't have. The churning, tumbling river, surging down at an incredible angle, made controlled navigation impossible. The heavy rolling of the water defined boulders lying submerged, waiting to break and crush any boat before drowning any creature so unfortunate as to be caught in the white water gauntlet. He and his brother were being dragged into those rapids and were about to be swallowed in a nightmare of splashing water.

The rapids stepped down sharply, as if it were one long cascading water staircase, twisted and broken. The thundering roar became a deafening monotone as they drifted nearer. Torrents of water jettisoned up like geysers then, crashed down again. Captured rays from the sun played in the mist, turning into rainbows shimmering mystically before their eyes.

"Heaven and hell," Rubin thought. They were captives of the current, facing a sentence of death by drowning. Rubin had paddled furiously to escape the bear, now he worked to escape the river. But it was too late. The strength of the river revealed itself as it tried to wrestle the paddle from his hands.

As the current sped them toward the rocks, Rubin recalled his training from the expedition. "Ride the rapids! Paddle to stay upright! Do not allow yourself to capsize!" Captain Lewis had issued those orders to the crew members as they struggled with their canoes in dangerous waters. Rubin didn't remember any situation quite like this, nor could he remember any advice about whirlpools, but he knew one awaited them at the end of this ride.

He carefully considered their predicament. Escape was impossible. They could only accept their fate and hope luck would carry them through. With odds of a thousand to one against them, his hands and arms began to cramp. His strenuous attempt to save himself and his brother was nearly at its end. A last-minute decision to submit to *Fate* gave Rubin a new, tranquil feeling. For a moment he recalled and reconnected with his feeling in the opening of the cave on the Lewis and Clark expedition.

Time seemed to stand still. His senses were keen. He felt no panic or fear. An unnatural sense of peace spread over him as he resigned himself to the end that called to him. His *destiny* lay before his eyes. The rapids would claim them both.

He knew *Fate* had conspired to send them to this place and time, and soon to their demise. Life is so strange. A person works hard, tries to do what's right, and look what happens.' He smiled then released a nervous giggle.

Seconds slipped by rapidly, yet he still saw things in a casual, slow-motion way. He recalled being in a similar situation with Lewis and Clark. The team had hiked around a stretch of white water. They named that place The Missouri Falls.

He remembered how formidable those rapids had looked to the team. They decided then to take an extra day to hike around the rapids. Just as he and Joseph had done the previous day. If this was the same cascading falls, then it was higher than its normal level. The extra water feeding into the river coming from the recent rains made it that way.

There had been no whirlpool the first time. But one waited for them now. If the rapids didn't kill them, the whirlpool surely would.

Joe was still busy trying to turn the anchor into a drag line to slow them and maybe, to pull them to the edge of the rapids. Rubin could see and understand all that lay before them. He no longer felt panicked.

He saw his brother looking at the same situation and knew he saw it as a threat, as the apocalypse of his life. It was obvious he would fight to the last moment. Rubin saw his brother, for the first time in his life, look worried and felt sorry for him. He wanted to call to him, "Just give in!" But he didn't.

Rubin knew they were *supposed to be here*. He knew without explanation that no amount of effort would change their *destiny*. He wondered if the bear attack had been part of a *divine plan* to place them here at this moment. He did what he believed anyone would do who recognized the power of their *manifest destiny*. He surrendered to it.

He could see his brother's face and the look of helpless alarm burning in his eyes. Rubin saw it all: The raging life-threatening rapids, the swirling whirlpool, the calm extension of the tail waters, and the bewildered expression on his brother's face. Their eyes locked on each other at the last moment. He smiled and closed his eyes as he felt the initial spray on his face. There was only a small bump as the muscular river flung the boat into the air, wrestling him quickly into dark, peaceful unconsciousness.

Coughing and choking, Rubin rolled over onto his side and vomited. He pulled himself onto his knees, physically stunned, mentally dazed, and shivering from the icy cold soaking he had taken. Slowly he tried to collect his thoughts. Trembling, he clumsily struggled to his feet. Barely standing, mostly staggering, he began to call out, "Joe . . . Joe!" Rubin could only hear the distant thunder of the rapids and the noise of the whirlpool.

In a panic, he looked up and down the river. He called out again and again for Joseph. The most violent section of the rapids lay about a hundred yards away, upstream. The rotating whirlpool stared at him like some kind of hungry eye.

He asked himself, how did I end up on shore? He looked around quizzically, finally noticing his hat at his feet. He had almost stepped on it.

Bending, he picked it up and placed it on his head. It was soaked and cold. Staggering, he wadded out into the river, oblivious to the biting chill of the water to call for Joe. Standing there with the river at his knees, just off the edge of the gravel and stone-strewn river bank, he heard voices. His pulse raced, though he stood frozen in step.

CHAPTER THIRTEEN

A rush of adrenalin shot through Rubin, making his hair feel like it was standing on end. He found himself staring at three young, though very serious-looking, Indian braves. They reminded him of vultures looking at their soon-to-be meal. The adrenalin rush made his senses peak. His muscles flexed and his breathing became short and rapid. He prepared himself mentally for a fight.

Quickly he tried to draw his knife. It was gone! They must have taken it, he thought. Or maybe he lost it in the rapids. And where was Joe? He looked around again, more frantically than before. "A weapon, I need a weapon." He vocalized his thoughts. Anxiety overwhelmed him. He thrashed his arms, twisting from side to side in an involuntary reaction to his predicament. He could find nothing to use as a weapon. He stood knee-deep in a river without a knife or gun while three Indians stared at him. He screamed out with frustration.

Rubin's spastic convulsions and loud words caused the young braves to jump nervously. His defense would have to be hand-to- hand. Just as he was about to regain enough composure to defend himself, one of the shy, frightened braves nervously took a small step forward and spoke a few words to him.

Rubin didn't understand the softly spoken, conciliatory words. Then cautiously, the young brave held out a knife in offering. It was his. Rubin sighed with relief and felt ashamed of him immediately.

He looked at the young braves through eyes that suddenly saw them differently. Fear and anxiety had blinded him. He began to laugh at himself, inwardly at first, then out loud. His laughter slowly turned into sobbing tears. He was alone, wet, and for a moment, scared half out of his mind. His emotions tumbled out of control. Here he was, on a mission to promote a better understanding between all people, and he had reacted defensively, with hostility.

He accepted his knife with a boyish grin and slid it back into the sheath that hung dripping wet from his side. He wiped the tears away and noticed the Indian boys carefully watching him. They were twitching like frightened puppies, looking as if they were prepared to take instant flight. Yet, they wouldn't flee. They had been taught to be brave and strong, at any and all cost to themselves.

Rubin wouldn't have blamed them if they fled or attacked him after seeing him react. Troublesome thoughts about dominant human behavior in various cultures ran quickly through his head. He, a man from a culture proclaiming itself as *civilized*, had acted *savagely*. These *"savages,"* proclaimed such by his culture, had acted *civilized*.

How and why did these people who lived with nature behave so peacefully? All the different people, all the different tribes, in many different locations, always seemed to be inquisitive and hospitable, although there were exceptions. Rubin and his fellow explorers had learned these people lived "the real life," the life *God* intended people to live. The white man lived a life in a reality he created. That was the difference and the problem.

Curious people of the woods. That's what the Lewis and Clark explorers called most of Native American people. They always seemed to be calm and rational. And he, who came from a so-called civilized culture, had reacted with hostility.

Using an apologetic tone, Rubin now spoke words of greetings to the young Indian braves. He knew they wouldn't understand what he said, but he felt compelled to say the words anyway. He was slow and deliberate with his words hoping they were intuitive enough to read his expression and tone. He did not want to sound hostile again.

"I'm sorry, I was frightened," he said calmly. He raised his right hand with the palm facing out. "Howdy! Believe it or not," he said with a more humorous tone, "I'm a peaceful man." His grin was contagious.

The young braves looked at each other quizzically, and then nodded their heads, smiling. They each raised their right hand, palm facing out, and said, "Ally."

"Ally," Rubin remembered meant "friend" in the Sioux language. That one word identified them and the general area he was in. Then he thought, are these people the *Dakota*, the *Lakota*, or the *Nakota*? They were all Sioux but each inhabited a different geographical area and they pronounced certain letters differently. He would pay attention, learning much by the way they spoke.

The three braves stood looking at Rubin who still stood in the river. Rubin, no longer felt threatened, stepped out of the cold river. He tried to tell these boys what happened and that his brother was missing.

He carefully said, "Joe is missing." They motioned for him to follow them. They led him along the shoreline to a large heap of broken sticks and soaked hides.

Apprehension gripped him when he realized he was looking at the remains of his canoe and his supplies. Quickly sorting through materials, he found his rifle. When he pointed the barrel down, a gush of water ran out. A little more searching revealed his waterproof powder flask and shot ball bag. But Joe was nowhere to be found.

Rubin once again became frantic. He tried to explain to these young braves that another person had been with him and was now gone. Over and over he said Joe's name until they seemed to understand. Spreading out, they all began calling for Joe.

He and the young braves, splitting into two groups, covered more than a mile of shoreline in an hour or so. Rubin was becoming hoarse from so much shouting. Finally, they met again at the wrecked canoe. The finality of the situation hit Rubin, he staggered. Joe's name still echoed in the river valley, cold as ice and twice as hard. The sound stabbed him. Then the echo settled into his soul and seized his heart like a vise. He desperately looked up and down the shore one last time before the devastating weight of harsh reality crushed him. He fell to his knees weeping uncontrollably. Joe was gone.

The young braves silently, slowly regrouped around him. Rubin composed himself but remained dazed by the trauma of losing his brother and nearly having lost his own life. The braves motioned for him to follow. He did so in a zombie-like trance.

They led him on a silent walk to their village. He couldn't think about anything other than Joe. The eyes of his mind remained focused on images of the moments just before they entered the rapids.

CHAPTER FOURTEEN

Shouts of fear and screams of terror ripped through the air. Rubin had a bad feeling deep in his belly. He knew events were about to get dangerous. The crowd of Indians squeezed around him. Escape was now impossible.

A menacing-looking brave, standing at least a head taller than the rest of the people, focused on Rubin and rapidly strode up to him. Stopping abruptly in front of him, he peered down through hate- filled eyes.

The three young braves stood close to Rubin as if trying to defend him. They chattered away. Rubin hoped they were trying to communicate to this beast that he posed no harm. With one quick, sweeping movement of his powerful arm, the murderous- looking brave brushed the three young braves aside. They tumbled to the ground in a pile, then picked themselves up and ran away.

"Thanks for the help," Rubin shouted after them, though rather softly. The braves rapidly disappeared. He felt compelled to say thanks to them despite knowing they wouldn't be able to hear or understand. Turning back to the tall Indian, he joked, "Nice place ya got here." He smiled broadly.

Rubin had a persistent, ingrained sense of humor.

On more than one occasion, others had found it annoying. Sometimes the things he said or did could have got him killed. Maybe this time might?

But try as he may to control his humorous tones, his lighthearted words tumbled from his lips before he could stop himself. He could only look up at the mighty brave, smile, then shrug his shoulders. He hoped the Indian would respond to his character, not his words.

The overly muscular Indian bellowed a curse, spat on the ground at Rubin's feet, then viciously grabbed him by the shirt with both hands and jerked him off his feet. He snarled through clenched teeth as he held Rubin nose-to-nose.

Rubin tried to remain calm though he trembled uncontrollably. He had been taught to never break a fixed stare with an Indian. In the Indian culture, that was not only disrespectful but could be construed as cowardly. That would expedite the person's demise. So he held the big Indian's piercing stare. Again, he smiled.

He tried to raise his right hand to give a peace sign but had it slapped down instantly. He was tossed back into the crowd as if he were little more than a rag doll. Now other unseen individuals seized him from behind, binding his hands behind him. He did not resist as they forced him to his knees. A knee pressed into his back as a strong hand viciously pulled back his hair. He was being bent like a bow about to be strung. His throat bulged out as it was exposed.

The big Indian waved a large knife in his face. The growling, insane-acting savage wanted Rubin to see what was to happen to him. He felt the edge of the blade press against his throat. With difficulty, he swallowed hard and began to pray.

Tense moments passed as the menacing Indian hesitated. Rubin's eyes had been closed tightly in prayer. Now he opened them — just a little — to see why the crowd suddenly calmed. The lethal slash of the blade was being reconsidered. Through his half-opened eyes, he saw his assailant look quizzically at his throat. He watched nervously as the big Indian carefully slid the blade under the medallion hanging around his neck. The gleaming knife's blade made a backdrop for a tarnished bronze medallion.

The strong, fierce brave struggled with a dilemma. He remembered medallions like the one Rubin wore. He just couldn't remember where he last saw it. Rubin had worn it since the conclusion of the Lewis and Clark trip. A peace medal, it was like others given to many of the Indians freely and with good will. Even the knife the brave carried could have been a gift bestowed on that trip! Now the medallion acted as a barrier for the hostile Indian's slashing knife. *Merciful Destiny* had interceded again.

Another Indian pushed through the crowd to get a better look at this new turn of events. This Indian acted a little more responsible and intelligent. Seeing the medallion, he turned quickly away, running and shouting, obviously looking for someone holding a higher position in the tribe. Rubin heard his shouts fade away as he disappeared into the crowd. He thought to himself, 'They know the medallion!'

"Thank you, *God*," he said softly. His prayers had been answered.

This giant, treacherous, knife-wielding Indian recognized the peace medallion of the Lewis and Clark expedition. Villagers began to grow more calm and quiet. The previously frenzied crowd, parted to provide a path for a beautiful young Indian woman. The villager who had left the scene in a rush a minute earlier now pushed her forcefully toward Rubin.

Rubin was helped to his feet. His bound hands were cut free. His hat was placed back on his head, backwards, by someone behind him. The woman stood before him. The villager held her by her shoulders, saying something Rubin didn't understand. She looked at the big Indian, who had nearly slashed his throat.

With fierce eyes she began to scold then slap at him. The crowd burst into laughter as that tremendously large and formidable brave backed away from this incredibly beautiful and delicate-looking Indian woman. He ran away and became lost in the crowd. Rubin sighed with relief.

She turned and looked straight into his eyes. "Forgive this man, please, he is much troubled." She spoke perfect French.

"I'm sorry ma'am, but I don't speak French." Rubin was sincere and embarrassed. He had several opportunities to learn French from Captain Lewis but thought it to be a waste of effort. His attitude now shamed him. He knew very well that French people had lived in this land for generations and, because of it, many Indians spoke French but not English.

"I speak —" she struggled for a moment searching for the word, and then continued with difficulty. "— English."

Rubin was enchanted by the woman, and flabbergasted that she knew any English at all. Her beauty stunned him. And her apparent power over the others made him feel safe. He looked long at his savior while massaging his wrists. Her hair was black as coal and straight as a taut string. It extended down to her breasts. That's where his gaze momentarily fixed. Her dark, exotic eyes were enchanting. The tight smile on her lips revealed a devilish character. She stood before him, hands clasped behind her.

After she studied him for a few minutes, she pointed to herself with both hands and said. "My name is Shadow."

Rubin quickly removed his hat as a gesture of respect. Then he stuttered as if he couldn't remember his own name. "It's my pleasure to meet you ma'am."

Then she spoke through her smile. "They say you are 'Man Who Stands in Water.'"

He could not prevent a smile from growing on his face. It felt like it reached from ear to ear. "My name is Rubin," he finally blurted out. "And sometimes I can speak all of one language."

They both smiled and searched each other with wondering eyes. The big Indian had not gone far and was working his way back to them. He noticed, with growing irritation, the interaction between Rubin and Shadow. He did not like it.

Growling like an angry bear, he pushed his way back to the front of the crowd. He grabbed Shadow by the arm, breaking the spell tying her and Rubin together. He scowled at her before he viciously backhanded her, knocking her to the ground.

Horrified, Rubin stepped quickly toward her. He reached to offer her aid but the big Indian grabbed him by the shirt once again pulling him back to a face-to-face position.

"You need to learn some manners," Rubin said through clenched teeth. He slapped his hands hard against the Indian's ears, popping his ear drums. Rubin fell to the ground as the big Indian released his grip on him to grab at his ringing ears. Rubin wanted to jump up and slug the big Indian but something told him not to. "Stay where you are and take advantage of the situation that presents itself to you," he heard his inner voice say.

The big Indian staggered and wove. He didn't give Rubin a target for a fist. Finally he stopped and leaned back in agony, still holding his ears. This put his chin way out of Rubin's reach. But right there, almost in Rubin's face, was the frontal bulge of the Indian's breechcloth. A solid uppercut to this most sensitive area made the Indian bend forward, bringing his chin within close range. "That's more like it," Rubin said as he stood up.

He pulled back and landed a solid fist on the protruding chin of the now crotch-grasping Indian. The Indian stiffened with eyes crossed, staggered back a few feet, and then fell spread eagled on his back. A cloud of dust erupted around him. He was knocked out cold.

The crowd, that only moments before cheered and jeered, now fell completely silent as they stared down upon the unconscious village bully.

Rubin shook his hand, checking for broken fingers. He quickly went to Shadow and knelt by her side. Gently, he put his arm around her. "Are you OK?" She did not answer. She only stared at him with adoring eyes. She was totally amazed. With a wet cloth he pulled from his pocket, he gently dabbed at her slightly bleeding lip. "We don't treat women like that where I come from," he told her sincerely. He helped her to her feet. Then she touched his cheek with her hand and smiled. He sighed.

CHAPTER FIFTEEN

Life with the Indians was difficult at first. But after a few weeks, Rubin felt safe, comfortable, and settled in the village. Being warmly accepted he decided to stay. Most of the villagers by then were comfortable with him too. Trust quickly developed, allowing all to feel safe and at ease with a white man amongst them. Besides, he no longer had a canoe for transportation.

Communication was almost impossible with anyone other than Shadow. But all the villagers enjoyed and looked forward to the constant game of charades he played to gain understanding. His relentless sense of humor kept everyone laughing at his overly dramatic acting game. And he enjoyed doing it as much as the others enjoyed seeing it. That is, all but one person, the big humiliated Indian. Though he stayed at a distance, he kept an eye on Rubin and Shadow.

The big Indian's name, Rubin eventually learned, was Angry Bear. He was the bully of the village and had been trying to win the attention and affection of Shadow for a long time, with no luck. To make matters even worse, his brother had been killed by a white man not long before Rubin was found and introduced.

Rubin reasoned the fear villagers exhibited when he first arrived was due primarily to that death. He understood Angry Bear's rage and realized friendship with him would probably never happen. Sooner or later though, they would meet again to have it out over Shadow, but he wasn't going to worry about it until it happened.

The atmosphere of the village was, for the most part, peaceful and well organized. Rubin liked it that way. The people living there were gentle and kind to each other and with him. He found no evidence of savagery. He witnessed remarkable parenting. Compassion and patience seemed to be *the code of life* in this tribe. Young adults and people who were not parents were, in fact, parenting other children when needed. Never once did he see the kind of discipline so prevalent in the white man's world.

All the people seemed to take special pride in giving aid to the elderly and the sick. Food was gathered from several sources and divided so all families got what they needed. No one was left out. After they got to know Rubin well, they were eager to help him any way they could. They had a good sense of humor, often laughing, taking life rather lightly, except one person. Angry Bear was always brooding.

Rubin noticed a remarkable difference of attitude in this culture. Excitement filled him as he thought he had discovered an Indian tribe that had a trait he could take away and spread beyond the borders of their land, and possibly this country. He prayed he was right as he considered the growth, the peace, the happiness and security that would propagate throughout the world as the contagion of this attitude captured all of humanity.

He found that people, who wanted to improve themselves in the eyes of others, would begin to treat other less fortunate people with favor. They would gather extra food or firewood for them and attended to most of their needs and wants. Rubin observed what he believed was true love between the practitioners of this custom and the recipients. It was an exercise that once started, never stopped. It only grew.

Shadow translated when no one could guess the charade Rubin tried to convey. She taught him bits and pieces of their language, as well as other things about their way of life, including the basic dos and don'ts, while introducing him to people and places. He tried to be a good student but had a hard time concentrating. Her beauty distracted him. Still, he showed progress. At the same time, he taught the villagers bits and pieces of the better parts of the white man's way of life. The exchange of information was good for all.

Thunder Horse, the Chief of the tribe was a kind, gentle, middle-aged man. He wore work clothes to pitch in with any group going about with their chores. His pride and joy — as with any Indian Chief — was a long, war headdress. The headdress wasn't really for war. It was, in fact, an article of clothing telling the story of the wearer's feats in battle and in war games. Good, honorable deeds done within the community were also reasons for feathers in the headdress. When a person could read the feathers and other adornments on the headdress, they learned much about the person who wore it.

There were no Friday or Saturday evening social events comparable to the white man's weekends. Special happenings arising during the day were enough excuse to have a Friday night-like community affair no matter what day it was. During these special nights the Chief could be seen walking around the village in his finest wardrobe. The villagers also wore their finest and stayed on their best behavior.

The Chief impressed Rubin as a man who listened patiently and then made intelligent decisions based on sound reasoning. He was very concerned about the message Rubin divulged.

"How did you learn of this?" asked Thunder Horse.

Rubin explained everything he could about the land east of the "Father of Waters," the Indian name for the Mississippi River. He tried to talk through the reasons the white man's government gave away Indian land. The hardest points to explain were the white man's set of values. Shadow did an expert job of translating for him, but she too, seemed confused about the intent of the white man's government.

"Are you sure that is how it is, are you sure that is what you want me to say? That makes no sense to me." She asked him with a troubled look on her face.

Rubin could only answer, "I know it makes no sense."

"Why would the white man wish to destroy our way of life?" the Chief asked Rubin. "There is enough for all in this great land. And why would the message of peace and prosperity brought by Lewis and Clark no longer be true?" He eyed Rubin with skepticism.

Burning Tree was the Shaman of the village. He sided with Thunder Horse and eyed Rubin with skepticism also. He posed most of his questions through Thunder Horse.

Rubin had a difficult time explaining the nature of the white man, particularly his politics. In trying to do so, he began to see and understand more completely the true nature of his culture. He became ashamed of his race, his culture, and his government for their audacity and greed.

He once thought the problems of the people; of his culture was the result of a poor ineffective government. Now he believed the problems of the people were of their own making. If they would be more vigilant about the actions of their government, more problems might be circumvented. He had no way to defend the actions of his culture.

He and Thunder Horse had many deep discussions about the true nature of the white man and the Indians. They discovered that many of their problems were very similar. Unnecessary battles about disputed land boundaries, livestock theft, and personal injustices led to long-lasting feuds. Rubin was horrified to learn some Indian tribes kept and bartered in slaves.

"People of *Maka*, Mother Earth, have many things to make better," Burning Tree said to Rubin. This was the first time the Shaman spoke directly to him. Thunder Horse nodded his head in agreement with Burning

Tree's statement. The more Rubin learned, the more he saw how their cultures suffered from problems of equal magnitude.

During these translated conversations, Rubin observed a wide range of emotions flashing over the Sioux Chief's face as recognition of cultural shortcomings became better understood. The Shaman was harder to read. Yet they all came to a similar conclusion: People were people no matter what their nationality.

Nodding in agreement, they recognized some people, for whatever reasons, reacted adversely at times. Some had dark motives; others were metaphorically "*touched by God.*" Most people though, just tried to get along and see the truth. They all smiled with relief at this revelation.

Both differences and similarities were apparent. Rubin could read confusion, compassion and concern in the Indian Chief's eyes. All the traits of a good human being, he thought. The Chief was very concerned about the future of both cultures, as well as being dedicated to doing his part to make a good future for all people living on *Maka*, Mother Earth.

Having won the acceptance of Thunder Horse and of the entire population of the village, less one, a council meeting was set up so Rubin could again try to explain the motivation behind his adventure. His sincerity and tenacity deemed worthy for special consideration. He would soon be able to discuss in detail, all the things he and his brothers thought would happen to the Indian nation in the near future.

Shadow was enjoying the process of learning things not known to most village women. Her life too, had become irreversibly changed by Rubin, the "*Man Who Stands in Water.*"

"I would like to know what this tribe calls itself," he asked her.

"We are the people of *Maka*," she responded.

"But you are a tribe of the Sioux nation. Do you call yourselves the *Lakota*, the *Dakota*, or the *Nakota?*"

She looked at him unable to understand why he needed to put a name on her people. But to satisfy his curiosity she answered simply, "We call ourselves *The Wooesa.*"

She smiled, turned and walked away. He looked after her with a slack jaw.

"I am here by the will of a Higher Power." He said to himself astonished.

CHAPTER SIXTEEN

Today Rubin was invited to sit and talk with Burning Tree inside his tipi. Shadow instructed him to look directly into his eyes when speaking.

"If Burning Tree sees deception or insincerity he will dismiss you by turning his head and ignoring you. He can answer many questions but you must speak from your soul." She told him firmly.

Rubin sat close to a small fire, as directed by Shadow. There was an animal hide partition dividing the tipi. Burning Tree wasn't present at the moment. Rubin looked at a buffalo skull that sat atop a round stone near the fire. In the dim light it looked like it still had eyes in its head.

Upon the hairless animal hide partition was a painting. Rubin strained his eyes to see in the dim light. His eyes widened with surprise as he recognized an unmistakable image.

He looked at Shadow and said excitedly, "I've seen a picture like that before."

"How is that possible, you have never been here?" She responded.

"I don't know how it is possible but I am telling you I've seen that picture before." As he looked back to reaffirm what he saw, Burning Tree was suddenly sitting there. Rubin could not prevent a gasp.

The Shaman studied Rubin with a penetrating stare for several minutes. Rubin narrowed his eyes to prevent himself from blinking as he returned the stare.

Without breaking the fixed gaze, the Shaman sprinkled something into the fire that made it momentarily flare up. Within that moment, a reflective pinnacle of light reflected in the Shamans eyes. It captured and took Rubin's soul hostage.

Rubin had been hypnotized by a blend of light and found himself once again falling or flying through the darkness. He steadied himself as the acceleration reached a speed he had yet to experience. He began to breathe deeply trying to control himself as best he could. He saw a small point of light in the darkness. It was approaching at a high velocity. He prepared himself for contact.

Then as quickly as it started, it was over. Rubin blinked and took inventory of his senses. Burning Tree gave a slow nod of approval. He spoke slowly so Shadow could translate.

"You have a troubled soul. You seek to know answers you think will solve problems only you and thinkers like yourself believe exist."

Rubin was breathing deeply, his heart thundered and he wanted a drink of water badly. Then a hand came from someone unseen behind him. It reached around him. It held a gourd cup full of water.

Soon after he drank, he calmed a little. Shadow translated as the Shaman spoke again.

"Our Shaman wants you to ask a question that will serve as one question to all."

Without taking time to think about it, Rubin asked. "I have been searching for a way to understand why so many problems have developed. It wasn't too long ago that I thought everything was good or was soon to be good for all people of the land.

Burning Tree stopped Rubin's rant by raising his hand and said, "Are you asking me why life seems so troubled after you thought all was well? Rubin tilted his head towards Shadow to listen to her translation as he kept his stare on the Shaman. And with just a slight smile on his lips he said, "Yep, I guess that's what I'm asking."

"Do you not want to know why there is good and bad? Do you not want to know why there is not one solution to fix many problems? The answer to all your questions is the same. You must improve your vision before you can see the answer.

Rubin thought of this before he replied. Then with confidence he asked several questions in succession. "Can we choose which path in life we should take, or are we destined by our circumstances and location? And are we able to change directions once we start our life's journey?

These were good questions, yet Shadow looked confused about the manner in which he questioned the respected Shaman. Burning Tree liked the questions and felt compelled to answer. He didn't seem perturbed at all by Rubin's tactics. The Shaman heard a soul call for help and he was going to help.

"We will lead you to the light. With the light you will be able to see. When you can see, all your questions will be answered. You must start with learning our way of life."

Burning Tree made a carful description. "Our way of life is structured around our tradition, and our tradition has developed from observations we take from nature, "The structure of nature is the will of *Wankan Tanka, The Great Spirit,* or as you and your kind will say, *God.* This way of life is so powerful that one like yourself must carefully consider if he truly wants to know the answers. Our people must know. They need to know to survive." He studied Rubin for a few long seconds before adding. "Do you truly want to know?"

With a worried look on her face, Shadow translated Burning Tree's statements.

"Be cautious, young white face. The answers to these questions will change your life forever." As Rubin contemplated this unexpected warning,

Burning Tree added, "No person is able to unlearn. The answers to these questions can be a heavy burden." The stern expression on Burning Tree's face bore testament to his serious attitude.

Rubin reflected back to a time while on the expedition, Joseph had asked. "Are you sure you want to know?" Rubin had inquired about certain circumstances within a tribe after having a private conversation with Captain Lewis. He was told that a young Indian maiden had been kidnaped from a rival tribe. She received very special treatment, including the best clothing and food. She was housed in a special lodge and treated with more respect and courtesy than any other member of the tribe. After about a month of this treatment, she was suddenly shot through the heart in the middle of a tribal ritual. She had been kidnaped, and then groomed as a sacrifice.

Up until this time, Rubin had experienced only the good nature of the Indians. He learned later that both captains were careful in selecting men who would see and learn about other cultures. This was a calculated move by them. Had the captains allowed all of the men to learn and witness these mortifying aspects of Native Americans, disastrous results could have ensued.

Few white men would have held a neutral position over such barbaric and primitive customs. Intervention from anyone though, could have been devastating to the success of the expedition, and ultimately, the nation.

Rubin believed the Indians incapable of what he called "white evil." With this one event, his illusion was shattered. Now he knew these people were just as capable of extreme savagery as the white people.

"People of all colors and of every culture are born into a life that only guarantees hardships and problems. This is a blessing. Basic survival is not even guaranteed." Burning Tree continued to answer Rubin's questions without giving him an opportunity to say he didn't want or need to know any more.

"It is these hardships and problems in our lives that create the atmosphere in which we learn to be good people. Think of it. Would it be better if we were born into a world that gave no reason to understand what makes all things work?" Burning Tree answered for him, "No, it would not. Death and suffering, in all forms and for all reasons, are there for us to witness and be a part of. All suffering and all deaths occur for good reason. Without hardships, we would never develop the character of good people. Best choices can only be made after a person has seen much, and much has been explained."

Rubin thought it was reasonable to assume this was what he and others of his culture called ageing.

The Shaman continued. "After many seasons of watching and learning a person usually figures out how to deal with problems successfully." The Shaman became quiet for several minutes. Rubin thought his meeting time was over.

Then he spoke again. "Some people take another path. Some who are strong enough and have satisfied spiritual qualifications can fly to the door of our *Creator, Wankan Tanka*. Only the strongest can go there and come back."

Rubin felt a tremor roll over his skin.

"Those who have been chosen to be explorers of the light are those who are on *Maka* with a mission. They receive powers meant to be tools."

Rubin was breathing hard again. He wanted to make an appeal to someone or something to excuse him from this responsibility. He tried to drink from his empty cup.

The Shaman said cryptically, "For many moons we have told a story about a man who will come. He is a man who has stepped from one life into the other. He will have the gift to see the will of *Wankan Tanka*. He will know how to listen and come back to save all by revealing a secret."

Then Burning Tree surprised Rubin by asking him a question. "Do we who are trying to do good know the intent of our *Creator?*"

Rubin swallowed hard before he could answer. "How would I know?" He said honestly confused.

Burning Tree finished by saying, "Some people think life must be always nice, kind, and pleasant or there is something wrong. It is that which is hard and unpleasant that make a person strong. It has been my observation that only the strong survive and thrive."

Rubin looked at Burning Tree in stunned amazement. Now he knew what Burning Tree meant when he said, ". . . a heavy burden of knowledge."

CHAPTER SEVENTEEN

Rubin awoke alone in his small tipi, glad the long, cold lonely night had ended. He welcomed the morning and the warmth of the day. Thinking of Shadow and knowing he would see her sometime during the day put a smile on his face.

The sun rose slowly into the clear morning sky, promising another hot arid day, although the early morning was still chilly. He got up, seeking a comforting fire and a morning meal.

He was not only free to wander about scrounging meals, it was expected of him. He was welcome at every tipi. Many times he laughed when he thought of how much he resembled a stray dog people adored, cared for, and fed. He held his head high in mocking self-adoration of his adopted role.

He returned to his favorite place for a meal. A large woman lived there. She made him a comfortable place by her outside fire and she told him he was always welcome. He called her "Large Woman" and teased and tickled her. She lost her husband and two sons many years ago and cherished his frequent visits, loving to feed a hungry man. He learned long ago that large women were usually very good cooks. And this large woman was not only a fantastic cook, but great company as well. She was as content as a woman could be who had lost all the men in her life.

After being thoroughly warmed and nourished, he began to relax. Quiet reflection, and a smoke provided by Large Woman, was a great way to end a meal and start the day. He was just beginning to enjoy the morning when the rapid chattering of curious village teens, and the equally intrusive barking of dogs, announced approaching company. He turned his head to see the small noisy group marching deliberately across the common area, coming straight at him. Burning Tree had summoned him.

A clearing near the edge of a high plateau provided the meeting site. Rubin had been taken there several times before to witness varied scenarios of nature. Overlooking a vast valley, where bison and antelope calmly grazed. This was a place where lessons of life could be observed. With the expansive vista, the location also functioned as a class room.

The younger braves who had yet to learn enough to be helpful on a hunt were sent here to watch and learn. At various times they could see wolves stalking the old and weak bison and antelope. Observant teen aged boys and girls pointed out predatory birds as they dove silently upon unsuspecting rodents. Coyotes, much more stealthy, were occasionally sighted by the more perceptive students. The feral canines had their own territory, separate from the wolves, and stalked jackrabbits and other rodents within the fallen rock area. Sometimes, groups of hunters were observed stalking their game, putting on a demonstration just for the benefit of their children.

The rising sun rapidly warmed the cool morning air. Most of the villagers had started their assigned duties. The women gathered wood or tended the gardens. Men separated into groups of herders, tool makers, and hunters. Everyone had a job.

Each day, Rubin observed the villagers getting on with their multitude of things to do. American Indians were not the savages spoken of back in St. Louis. These were intelligent, organized people with a purpose and goal for every day. But today, Burning Tree summoned him for what he expected to be another day of philosophical discussions on the way of Indian life and the predictable methods of nature. He enjoyed these discussions. They not only opened his physical eyes and ears, but his inner senses as well. He felt his life changing from the understanding he gained at every meeting.

Rubin's escorts stopped close to the old Shaman. They bowed to Burning Tree, and then made a hasty retreat. Burning Tree was not alone. Shadow was standing near, looking out over the open valley. She turned and looked at him. Her eyes were dark, penetrating, and exotic. She held his gaze for a few seconds before she flashed a quick devilish smile. It was just long enough to enchant him. He wondered if she knew what she did to him. Quickly, she checked her smile and turned her attention to Burning Tree.

The slow wave of his hand toward a basket at her feet was a silent command to serve drinks from the crocks held within. She knelt, folding her legs under her, before sitting on them. Rubin and Burning Tree remained standing. Using both her hands, she handed a cup to the old Shaman. Then she did likewise with Rubin. He reached for it, trying to take it from her, but she held onto it for just a moment to distract him before releasing it. A smile crossed her lips as his eyes met hers. His heart raced as he looked down upon her smiling face and into her dark eyes.

She turned her attention to Burning Tree. The Shaman spoke and Shadow translated as she stood up again.

"We, *the Real People*, live by the laws *Wankan Tanka* has made.

Wankan Tanka speaks to us in the language of the sacred life." He opened his arms as if revealing the vista dominating their view. "*Wankan Tanka* speaks to us through the actions of the land and all that live here. We see pain, suffering, denial, and death, and understand they are necessary to keep our spirits sensitive."

He and Shadow stopped and looked at him to see if he understood. He nodded his head to indicate, "Yes." Then Burning Tree continued.

"If our spirits lose that sensitivity, then we will cease to exist. It is the power that lays hidden within the realms of suffering that opens our eyes and ears. As it is with the antelope, to survive one must keep eyes and ears sharply tuned. Relaxation causes slowed reaction time and weakness of the body. Rubin wanted to ask questions but felt it best to just listen and observe.

"Change is all that is constant." Burning Tree motioned to a small group of boys climbing over a large stone. "I was once a small boy with many questions and much energy." He paused for a long minute as if held captive by the memory. Then he said, "Now I am an old man with less energy and only one answer." Rubin cocked his head anticipating a good follow up.

"Life will be the way it should be regardless of our intentions or devices. Despite what your culture or my culture may think about our progress, we can only do and accomplish what we are predestined to do." The Shaman paused for a long moment before continuing. "Don't confuse destiny with limitations of a mind process that has not yet fully developed."

Rubin's eyes flicked back and forth searching his memory for a meaning to this statement. He quickly thought about all the things he had been doing to change what he believed was the immediate future. Then he remembered the mural in the cavern and the art work on the animal hide in the Shamans tipi.

The changes the expedition caused were the first examples entering his mind. The Shaman stepped closer making Rubin nervous. "People who can see only with the eyes in their head and not with the eyes of their soul will miss seeing the true intentions of *Wankan Tanka.*"

The reality Rubin knew and the reality Burning Tree knew were two different realities. Burning Tree could read the confusion in his eyes. He turned away and looked out into the valley. Shadow followed and motioned for Rubin to pay close attention.

They watched as two hunters walked up to an antelope they had just killed. Burning Tree pointed to the hunters. "What do you see?"

"I see two hunters who have just made a kill," he said with a smile, thinking he had observed and proclaimed correctly.

"Do you not also see people who will be well fed by this animal? Do you not also see the triumphant hunters applying what they have learned over many hunts to make this kill possible? Do you not also see the life this animal led, bringing it to this time and place by the direction of *Wankan Tanka*? The Sacred path this animal has lived will continue in the people it nourishes. Do you not also see the life cycle that is before you?" Burning Tree finished with a tone of defiant certainty. "Death and life are supposed to balance each other." Rubin's smile quickly fell.

"The eyes of a sensitive soul see the complete story of life." Burning Tree added after noticing that Rubin's eyes were now really open. "Being able to see with the eyes of your soul will allow you to see the path *Wankan Tanka* has arranged for you to journey upon. This is a sacred path that will keep you nourished and peaceful. Then all will be well." Rubin nodded his head. He could indeed see more clearly now.

He believed he would see all things more completely from now on. Shadow could read the look of understanding in his eyes. She smiled with approval.

CHAPTER EIGHTEEN

Burning Tree reintroduced Rubin to nature and to life among the people who called themselves the *Wooesa*. Being familiar with traditions and customs was required before an individual could be brought before the tribal council's attention. Positive mystical readings from Burning Tree, plus other natural qualifications, such as humility, sincerity, and the ability to forgive, impressed Burning Tree and Thunder Horse. Rubin was true of heart and wanted to help make life better for all. This bought him acceptance with favor. A council meeting was arranged so he could impart his message.

Shamans, Sachems, and Chiefs, normally excluded women from participation in council meetings. Women of this culture knew tribal rules. Most women made their opinions and desires known through the men in their lives, their fathers, brothers, and uncles. But the rare and unusual circumstances and the troubling subject matter required Shadow to translate for him. He believed his message was vital to the very existence of all the native peoples of this land.

It had only been a few days since the meeting with Burning Tree on the edge of the plateau. Rubin remembered well, overlooking the hunting scenarios and watching teachers teach and children learn. He now stood with Shadow before the assembled council.

The assembly consisted of Chief Thunder Horse, Shaman Burning Tree, and several older men who served as the seers of the village. They sat on animal hides of exceptional quality and color patterns.

Thunder Horse spoke simply, "Tell us words from your heart." Rubin directed his words to Shadow's ear, saying, "Tell them I have seen the people of *Maka* riding away into the heavens."

They stirred nervously and became noticeably irritated as Shadow translated. She continued, "Rubin has also seen the blood of many white men and many of the *Real People* flowing over the land."

She translated the reasons Rubin gave for future battles with the white man. Disorder erupted. Confusion over past and current messages disrupted their beliefs. "The future is full of trouble but solutions are possible," Shadow shouted at the council.

Several minutes passed before order restored itself. Individual debates between council members quieted. Shadow began to relax. Rubin sighed and said, "Now I have to tell them the bad news. I have been to this land of the *Real People* before." He held out the peace medal for them to see. They held out theirs for him to see. "OK, you know my previous history. The message we brought," he paused for a long time, trying to think of the best way to explain the lie without saying the expedition members lied to them.

He took a deep breath and said, firmly, "The message brought to the people of this land by the Lewis and Clark team, "was a lie." The council members erupted once again with harsh words calling Rubin a liar. Shadow frantically tried to keep up with the translations.

He was trying to control the situation before it became explosive. "I don't believe it was a deliberate lie," he shouted. "We, the members of the Lewis & Clark expedition and the captains themselves, believed we were telling the truth. Believe me when I say we thought we brought a message of truth. But the truth has changed." This statement was troubling for the Indians.

Rubin tried desperately to explain himself but ended up feeling he had failed his brothers and the Real People of the country. "Oh Joe, if only you could have been here." He said dejectedly to himself. The only comfort he got from the meeting was the explanation Shadow gave him. "They are disturbed because they know of many lies the white man has said throughout time." Rubin was listening to her with interest. "There was a time when our people lived closer to the rising sun." She pointed to the east. "Many, many, moons ago a great white father made a promise. He lived over the water that takes many, many moons to cross."

Rubin assumed she was referring to a King from England, probably a hundred years or so before. Maybe it was an emissary from Spain or Italy, where the skin color is darker, closer to that of the Indian.

"That great father said white people would never come to our land." She paused and looked at Rubin for a long time. "White man came, killed many of our people, and took our land. My great, great grandparents are buried in high land that I have never seen, my mother and father have never seen." She looked toward the east as if she were trying to see the Allegheny Mountains, over seven hundred miles away.

He instinctively took her hand. "I'm so sorry for the trouble the white man has caused you and your people." He was so close to tears his voice cracked and trembled, making it very hard for him to speak. He gave up trying and quickly walked away, ashamed of his race and culture. He knew, in the next few years, white men would do much more harm to these people. The admission made him physically ill. His heart ached for Shadow and her people. His soul cried out to God for mercy for all the natives of America.

He sat alone by the fire he made under the stars without tipi or other shelter, farther away from the village than he had camped before. He was being tormented by new knowledge of wrongs done to these people.

He and the Lewis and Clark team, including both Captains, had been used by the government, either deliberately or unintentionally, to make peace with the natives to persuade them to go along with a plan that would reorganize the entire nation of native peoples. He scolded himself for not seeing past the ideology of an infant government and the patriotic pride he and the other members of the Lewis and Clark team held. He remembered what Burning Tree said about intentions and devices, about destiny and a thought process that had not yet fully developed in man. He was deeply depressed, in much the same manner as Captain Lewis.

He sat for hours brooding over the hurt he knew he had caused. The look on the face of Burning Tree told him he would never be truly trusted again. And Thunder Horse . . . He looked ready to declare war on all white people. "What can I do?" he called out in anguish.

Shadow had said this council session was only a preliminary event. It was meant to see if a meeting with other more important Chiefs and Shamans was warranted. He hoped he hadn't destroyed his chance to convey his message.

Shadow stood unobserved in the darkness watching him. She was convinced he had properly seen the future. Frightened by his vision, she was still infatuated with him. She wanted to go to him, but held back. She wanted to comfort him, but did not know what to say. So she stayed in the darkness peering at him with her dark eyes sparkling like stars in the heavens.

CHAPTER NINETEEN

Rubin was again summoned by the Shaman. He walked rapidly from the far edge of the village, having grown familiar with the ritual. He recognized in himself considerable growth, both spiritually and intellectually from the meetings with Burning Tree. He smiled with satisfaction over his new found confidence and life change.

Learning about Indian life, and more importantly, learning about the contrast between the two life styles he knew, gave him particularly useful insights about how and why people behaved the way they did. These meetings with the Shaman were also a perfect opportunity to get closer to Shadow.

Today he met her midway across the common area. They both walked briskly with their escorts, the village children. The air was warm and the sky clear. Shadow watched him. Her hair brushed softly against her face as a gentle wind stirred. The breeze would have gone unnoticed had it not been for her hair revealing its presence. The small things he noticed were now making the biggest differences in his life.

He watched her looking at him and wondered what questions lurked behind her eyes. What stirred in her beautiful form?

A trip across the continent and lengthy discussions with men of higher learning had prepared him for an incredible future. But still he was short on knowledge of the most sought after knowledge known to mankind. He wanted to know about women. He looked at Shadow and knew there was something unique and powerful about her. Something about her made everything he did seem to have more value. He had come to believe that there was something in most women that held all of humanity together. A smile from her and a look into those dark eyes had become his most sought after gift.

As he stood before Burning Tree he contemplated the lessons he had learned and the lessons he was about to learn. But it all became less important to him at this moment. He only wanted to know about Shadow. She smiled at him and flashed her sparkling dark eyes. He was now hopelessly focused on her. The thoughts he held and his growing desire for her ended when Burning Tree bellowed loudly, breaking the spell.

"We, the children of *Maka*," he said as he spread his arms to include their surroundings, "are on the path to our destiny." The old Indian spoke slowly and chose his words carefully. Shadow translated with great care and feeling. "Our destiny is to suffer from the hands of the white man until we are no more. We, *The Real People*, will lead the way for all the people of *Maka*, for all the ages, to understand how to live. Our example of living and dying will inspire future peoples to respect, revere, and save *Maka* from being stripped of everything that makes her mystical and powerful.

Rubin tried hard to focus on what the Shaman said but was averted by his words mystical, and powerful. He also heard the word her, as the Shaman spoke of *Maka*. He looked at Shadow again. Then he had an epiphany. The earth, *Maka* gives life. His mother, Viola gave him life. And Shadow has given him a new life. His body became slackened and he swayed almost falling over. His mouth hung open as the profound meaning of woman became perfectly clear. He looked at Shadow with reverence. Rubin interrupted Burning Tree to proclaim his new discovery, "*Wankan Tanka*, that is God to us white people, is female." Shadow looked at him with surprise as she translated.

Burning Tree was silent as he reassessed Rubin. Shadow too reassessed him. Then she pushed him hard and scolded him. "I am a woman only, nothing else!" Burning Tree reassessed her.

A few awkward minutes passed before the Shaman resumed his oration about the reasons for the conflict of cultures.

Then he finished by saying, "the buffalo will be plentiful, and the water will never run dry. We will dance around the fire, and the white man will not be able to disturb our peace."

It took Rubin several minutes before he could clear his head of the profound meaning of woman he knew was correct. Then he asked Burning Tree, "Are you speaking for all *The Real People of Maka?*" He knew tribes and clans of varied cultures existed all over the world, some yet to be discovered. He waited for an answer but got none. Then he tried to impress the Shaman with the need to do something more aggressive and less ideological.

"This Shaman needs to convince others they should try to save themselves." He complained to Shadow. "Tell him to organize the various tribes and clans, send representatives to Washington to argue for all the Real People, or retreat to a safer place," he pleaded. He only stopped his impassioned rant because he noticed the old Shaman seemed to not care about the white man's way.

"Are you telling him properly what I'm saying?" he asked. Shadow, noticed a puzzled look on his face, and then nodded emphatically.

Burning Tree continued after he was certain Rubin had finished making his point. "The plan of the *Creator* is to teach the people who do not live by the design of *Maka* that their way of life is wrong. After many seasons have come and gone, and after all *The Real People* are gone and after many white faces have died by the hands of other white faces, only then will they have learned. They will see and feel the pain of all the souls that have met their demise by the hands of the white man. It will take many generations to pass before enough misery has been made by the white man before he can see. This will make the white man sensitive.

This is what the white man needs and only after this has happened will they learn how to be sensitive. Only then will they be able to fulfill their destiny. Only then will their souls be real and free."

"The white man must have a powerful and sensitive soul to fulfill his destiny," Burning Tree said. He paused for a long time and watched Rubin closely to see if he understood.

Rubin asked, "What is the destiny of the white man?"

Burning Tree threw back his head and spread his arms wide as if revealing the sky to Rubin. "*The heavens,*" he bellowed. His words bounced off the distant bluff and made an eerie echo. The Shaman's words and the scream of a soaring eagle blended in perfect harmony.

The Shaman continued rapidly with uncharacteristic enthusiasm. "Only with a sensitive and powerful soul will the white faces know the sacred value of life. Then they will know how to connect to the other side. The other side will have the key to the heavens."

Rubin thought on this for a few minutes, wondering if the old Shaman spoke metaphorically.

"The white faces will ride birds of fire into the heavens," Burning Tree continued. "That is where the destiny of the white faces will be."

Rubin stood in stunned amazement at this revelation. Yet he had seen it before. It came back to him in an instant, the ancient mural in the cave with the white faces painted on stick like figures and the flaming birds with white faced figures riding into the heavens. He looked into the dark eyes of the old Indian, then into the vast blue sky. He could see an eagle soaring between the formless white clouds. He had seen this image before too, in the eyes of a dying Indian. He began to ask if the eagle was a gatekeeper or something similar, but as he looked back at Burning Tree, he saw clouds drifting in the old Indian's eyes.

The eagle screamed again.

CHAPTER TWENTY

Rubin, with his new appreciation for the people he had been living among, busied himself trying to learn as much as he could about the people who had saved his life. These kind and compassionate people had nurtured him and refreshed his spirit. He no longer felt dislocated. His fear and apprehension had been replaced with a feeling of kinship.

Losing Joe had been the most difficult situation he ever had to deal with, devastating in so many ways. Joe had always been there as a big brother and a father figure. He had guided his brother Gus and himself through most of their lives.

He had nurtured their inquisitive natures, creating a safe range of opportunities for their learning. As Rubin thought back on past events, he remembered many times how Joe had made personal sacrifices for them, the kind of sacrifices normally expected of a father. He even took care of neglected chores to save his "sons" — his brothers — from the wrath of their mother. Now he was gone. The void in Rubin's life could never be filled.

He had given some thought to abandoning their mission. Yet, in his heart, he felt as though Gus and Joe were still with him, giving silent encouragement to his soul, as well as an undefinable feeling of security. He would carry on.

He considered, for a brief time, a trip home to regroup. But he changed his mind after admitting he cared for Shadow too much. He also cared for all the people she called "*tiyospayes*," the Sioux name for family and close friends. He had to carry on for all these people. After all, they were the reason for the mission in the first place, and the mission was still important to the future of the Native Americans. He reminded himself the mission was also crucial to the future of his culture as well.

"We will make a better path for all of humanity to follow." That haunting phrase, if nothing else, would keep him focused.

Joe would have insisted he continue with the mission. It was too important for so many different reasons. So Rubin made a new commitment to follow through with the plan he and his brothers had originally envisioned. Only now he would serve alone.

Rubin had always been dependent on Joe, maybe too dependent. His brother would have taken control of this and any other situation that arose. He never considered being the one in the lead role. Joe had been the thinker, the planner, the doer. Now Rubin had to follow through for him. It was going to require more from him than he thought he would ever have to give.

He had to rearrange his priorities. First he had to do something about his communication skills, or lack of them. Something could happen to Shadow, as something had happened to Joe. This made him stop and consider once again how important she was to him. He reflected back to Sacajawea. She was the key to holding everything together on that expedition. Now Shadow was the key. He sat down to meditate on this and noted with certainty how women held the fabric of humanity together.

He had learned, through observation and by listening, that men thought themselves in charge of the destiny of their families, communities, and even the world. But that was all an illusion. Men survived on their egos. Women made everything work, despite men.

"Another priority to set and live by," he said to himself, "bring good women into my life and listen to them. I won't have any problem remembering that. That, all by itself, will make this mission work."

He knew Joe had a special way of interacting with people. Joe had always been slow and gentle, never pushy or overbearing. People liked him and listened to him. And Joe listened to people. He looked at them and really listened. Rubin needed to work on his listening style and to try harder not to make inappropriate, humorous remarks. "That will be the hard part," he told himself with a wry smile.

With a renewed commitment to his mission, Rubin put his plan in order. First and most importantly, he had to return to the river. He had something urgent to do.

Days later, he secretly and quietly walked back to the river where he lost his brother. He had to be alone for this knowing it would be painful. The thought of confrontation with his real feelings frightened him. But he knew he needed to openly grieve. He had to get it all out. He had to say good bye. Only then could he get on with his life and on with the mission.

Standing on the shore, he recollected being saved by the young braves that were now his good friends. Some of the remains of the canoe were still there, splintered, piled and useless. He stared for a long time, mesmerized. It hurt to look upon the slowly decaying debris.

The wood frame was bleached white from exposure to the sun. The hides had been carried away by scavengers. He had an urge to bury everything that was left. "Later," he told himself. Slowly he paced in a small area holding his hat in his hands. Then he stopped, faced the river and stared at the gentle, drifting current. It was no longer a menacing torrent. The current had slowed and the river level was down several feet. The whirlpool was gone, too. It was as if all those things conspired to put him there at that time. It was the will of *Wankan Tanka*. He drew in a deep breath.

"Joe," he called out. An eerie echo was the only reply. The distant, softened roar of the rapids sounded like a chorus of angels. It chilled him to the bone. "I'll carry on," he said, his voice had grown deeper and more mature. "Your brothers will always miss you, and I'll always . . ." He struggled to finish the statement. "I will always love you."

He never told his brother he loved him. It seemed too unmanly then. Now he considered it an act of real manhood. Regret for never saying this little phrase flooded him with sorrow. He hung his head and struggled to retain his composure. Many of the personal things Joe told him throughout his life mystically echoed in his head. He lost his composure and feel to his knees weeping with total abandon.

Two dark eyes peered at him from around a tree. Shadow suffered quietly with him. Her tears flowed. It took all her self-control to keep from running to him, to hold and comfort him, to cry with him. She saw him stand up, raise his head and put his hat back on. He wiped his face. She ducked back out of sight, concealing herself and her growing affection for him.

Later in the day, with the sun high and the day bright, Rubin put the finishing touches on a short message he carved on a small piece of wood. He had been quiet for several hours. Shadow kept a respectable distance, knowing he needed time and space, but she stayed close enough for translating services, should he need her. Joe had triggered in him, deep emotional thoughts of family and the love between them. He was motivated to try and communicate with Gus and Rachel.

A piece of wood, a panel from a small crate from his salvage scrapes, was all he could find for the message. The panel piece was less likely to be destroyed or distorted. He gave careful thought to the content of the message. There wasn't much room on the small piece of wood. The few words he carved into the slat carried a powerful statement, though. *"Have found peaceful people to spread message."* The finishing touch was a rough cut of his name. He was very careful not to write anything that might cause panic or worry. He had considered carving the words, "to help me." Instead, he carved, "spread message." Any clue referring to him as being alone might cause anxiety for Gus and Rachel.

He wanted to put Joe's name on it, but was glad he ran out of room. It was all he dared to send back, just enough to alleviate the anxiety he knew must be burdening them. Maybe he could send another message at a later time, he told himself. But for now, this would have to suffice. The story about Joe needed to wait for a face-to-face explanation.

In the village, he examined the carefully carved piece of wood one more time before handing it over to a young Indian brave.

"Yumni," he said, a serious look on his face, "it's in your hands now, my friend." Yumni, of course, looked to Shadow for the translation. Rubin was confident his message would be taken downstream to Gus and Rachel.

He watched with admiration as the sturdy-looking Indian brave set out on foot, taking with him only a few provisions. The brave beamed with pride for having been selected to go on this very important mission for the 'Man Who Stands in Water.'

He would have to live off the land and hope to encounter at least a few hospitable villages along the way to nourish and help him, if needed. And in the young brave's possession was the most important message Rubin had ever sent.

CHAPTER TWENTY ONE

The evening meal had just concluded. Steaming coffee filled the room with a relaxing aroma. Rainier patted his swollen belly and rose from the table. Thanking and praising Rachel for the wonderful meal. He excused himself, saying he had a few chores to do before turning in. "I got to stock the wood ifin we be gonna stays warm this night." He and Gus nodded to each other. It was a man's way of saying loose ends were being tied up for the night and all was well. Then Rainier stepped outside.

Rainier shared every meal with Gus and Rachel at their table. At first he felt awkward with this arrangement, but soon found it easy to sit with and share meals and conversation with them. Until he met the Fields, he had never sat at a table to share a meal with white people. Things like that were not done where he came from.

The Fields had insisted from the beginning that he share their home with them. They all worked together to fix up a room and give it some furnishings despite protests from Rainier. It was the first time he ever had a room of his own, but Gus and Rachel considered him one of the family.

After Rainier had stepped outside Rachel began her kitchen cleanup ritual. Gus slipped his suspenders down off his shoulders, and rolled a cigarette. This was his time to unwind and really enjoy domestic living.

The peace and tranquility were suddenly shattered when they heard Rainier shout out, "Gus, come quick, we gots company!"

Rachel's eyes flashed at Gus, showing him the alarm she felt upon hearing Rainier's serious tone. Gus crossed the room in three long steps. He grabbed the rifle hanging loaded and ready over the door. Jerking the door open, he bounded out onto the porch.

It was early evening and shadows were growing long. There wasn't much light left, but there was enough for Gus to see. The only sound came from a few cackling chickens scratching around on the bare ground before they went to roost.

Gus stood with rifle in hand, the unlit cigarette in his mouth, his suspenders dangling. His eyes followed the path of Rainier's steady stare. Rainier stood frozen in his tracks just a few yards away from the bottom of the porch steps. Gus's eyes locked on the image of Rainier's alarm.

Standing about twenty yards away in the gateway of the flimsy split-rail fence, was a young Indian brave. He seemed to be studying the gate lying to one side off its hinges. His casual demeanor reflected peaceful self-assurance. He turned his face up slowly to look at Gus and Rainier. He showed no fear, even though he was looking at a man who held a long rifle. A snort from a palomino in the coral drew the Indian's attention. He was without a horse.

Arrow feathers protruded over one shoulder from the quiver on his back. He held his bow in one hand at his side. A large, sheathed knife rode on one side of his waistband while a tomahawk hung loosely from the other side. Yet, he didn't appear to be a threat.

Gus calmly lit his cigarette and slowly pulled his suspenders up onto his shoulders without ever once taking his eyes off the athletic-looking Indian. "Don't break eye contact, that is considered disrespectful, and never show fear. Don't stand frozen or make any rapid movements." He recalled the words and tone of his brother. Joe knew Indians, Gus did not. "Act natural and move slowly."

Stepping down off the porch, Gus stood next to Rainier. "What you think, Gus?" Rainier asked in a nervous whisper.

Gus took another puff off his smoke, then handed Rainier his rifle. Rainier's eyes widened with fright and disbelief. His expression was so comical that had Gus not been so concerned, he would have laughed.

"Just watch him close. Okay?" He winked at Rainier and slapped him on the shoulder, then walked toward his visitor. He stopped about halfway between the Indian and the house. His hands hung at his side with palms open. He was making it obvious he was without any weapons. He spoke over his shoulder to Rainier; "Don't do anything unless I say so!"

"Yes, sur," Rainier replied.

Gus raised his right hand up with the palm out. He didn't try to speak any of the Indian dialects he knew for fear of offending, so he spoke in English. "Hello, you are welcome here."

"Ally." That was all the Indian said as he held his right hand up, palm out. Gus wasn't sure but he thought "ally" meant friend or friendly.

The Indian brave crouched down slowly and laid his bow on the ground. Standing up, he drew his knife from its sheath and his tomahawk from his waistband. He dropped them to the ground. With a swinging motion, he pulled the quiver off his shoulder and laid it carefully next to his bow. Holding his right hand up, palm facing forward, he walked up to Gus. Then he very slowly lowered his left hand down to his legging and pulled a thin piece of wood from a side pocket and offered it to Gus. It looked like a small piece from a wooden crate. Gus looked at it quizzically. It had words carved on it.

The humble household celebrated more from the heart than from substance. Gus had no liquor but did have a bottle of wine he had saved for a special occasion. This rated as a special occasion. Rachel prepared a little of everything in an effort to satisfy the endless hunger of the Indian brave. He ate like a starved dog.

Neither Gus, Rachel, or Rainier spoke the language of the Indian. And he didn't speak theirs. But there was one word, one single word, a name spoken and understood by all. They said it over and over again. This single word brought laughter, tears and cheers. The single word was, "Rubin." They even sang a single name song. Rubin, Rubin, Rubin. Rainier played his harmonica and they all sang that single word song. Rubin, Rubin, Ruuuubin.

Rubin was alive and, as far as they could guess, he was well. They all studied the small piece of wood, held it close as if it had been anointed by divinity and possessed holy powers. Rachel pressed it to her face and with her eyes closed tight; she looked as if she was in some kind of spiritual communication.

Introductions were always easy. People had only to point to themselves and utter their names. The young Indian's name was Yumni.

Rainier played his harmonica much to Yumni's amusement and amazement. Gus danced carefully with his very pregnant wife. Yumni had eaten so much his belly was as big as Rachel's, and he was still eating. Their simple celebration went long into the night.

They may not have understood one another's words, but they did understand the joy of knowing Rubin. He was still alive. After a cup of wine, Yumni had become very bold with Rainier. He had obviously never seen a black man and was determined to understand how and why he had black all over his body.

Rainier was patient and tried to explain that it was only skin color. The one-on-one encounter Gus witnessed brought back memories of the stories Joe and Rubin told about York and his Indian encounters. Gus wondered how similar York and Rainier might be.

Rainier went on to explain there were actually three different colors of people present. Then he said, "But we all be the same color inside." Gus and Rachel were touched by Rainier's heartfelt explanation, and they believed

Yumni understood at least some of what he said. A spiritual bonding took place between the four of them.

Gus, like his brothers, believed skin color had no bearing on a person's personality or capabilities. Spirituality had no color and the spirit moved the bodies of all people regardless of skin tone or gender. He too felt the mild effects of the wine and drifted into a philosophical state of mind. He would, later that evening, spend some time alone, outside, gazing up into the star-filled sky, communing with *God*.

With the coming of morning, their guest seemed eager to begin his long trip back from where he came. Rachel had prepared a large bag stuffed with all sorts of things for him to eat on his return trip. He was chewing on something that very moment. Gus had written a rather lengthy letter telling and asking Rubin all sorts of things. One of his questions was about Joe. He was sending along with Yumni several pieces of writing paper and a quill with a small packet of dried ink. He and Rachel hoped somehow, a correspondence system could be worked out.

Departure was from the same place where Yumni had arrived, at the front gate. Rainier gave Yumni his harmonica as a gift. Yumni immediately blew into it, with much delight. Rachel made her offering of good eats and added a big hug that somewhat bewildered him.

Gus motioned for him to wait while he ran off to the barn. He quickly returned with a bridled palomino horse. He put a saddle blanket on the horse knowing Yumni would appreciate it much more than a saddle.

The overly-excited Indian brave began to yelp and howl with delight. Without understanding exactly what he was saying, Gus got the jest of it. Yumni seemed to be praising the heavens, earth and all things in-between for this blessing. Gus stepped back when he had calmed down and bade him farewell with raised hand.

Yumni stepped back then easily mounted the horse. He gave a long farewell speech that no one understood, then turned his horse and rode away.

They all waved and watched him disappear into a thicket of woods. Rachel sighed deeply. Gus hugged her tightly with one arm around her and said, "All is well." He looked up to the blue sky. "I thank you *God*, for this messenger bringing us word from my brothers."

CHAPTER TWENTY TWO

Rubin looked dumbfounded and asked Shadow with a questioning tone. "*Man with Important Messages?* I thought I was *Man Who Stands In River.*"

"*Man Who Stands In Water.*" Shadow Corrected. "You have two names now, is big honor." She said smiling.

"Clan woman give you second name after Yumni get blessing."

Yumni sought a customary blessing from the clan woman before leaving to take an important message to Gus and Rachel. She then bestowed Rubin with another name. *Man With Important Messages.*

With the honor of a second name, Rubin began to notice people regarding him more respectfully. They did that by having the privilege to say his name. Some people would walk from the farthest point of the village just to have a chance to see him. Hopefully they would cross his path enabling them to say his name, preferably being witnessed by many. With every honor he enjoyed, he never failed to praise Shadow in his own way. She was responsible for everything good. She stepped in and saved him from mutilation by a disturbed brute immediately upon his arrival. She made every translation passionately.

He loved to watch her doing her work. She was athletic and young, focused and strong. She had become an extension of himself. He trusted her too. Many times she had conferred with him before translations were made. She would suggest other words or metaphors. Everything he enjoyed, she made possible. She made him think and feel differently about his life. His senses had been awakened and were reshaping his life. Rubin was slowly developing into, *A Real Person*.

Other favorable considerations included a position as a guest listener at council meetings and opportunities to meet with governing heads of other tribes and clans. He was informed that his word had been spread to the farthest western point of land on the continent. Word had come back that interested Chiefs and Sachems included a legendary Shaman named Mountain Wind. Rubin surmised that Mountain Wind was as close to a saint as could be achieved in the Indian culture.

Shadow told him that she had overheard people talking about a journey Mountain Wind would take him on.

This made Rubin think he might have to leave with others with higher authority. He looked at Shadow and asked her, "Do you think my time here may be ending?" He reached out to her and gently stroked her arm with his finger.

"I would not like to see you go." She said quickly looking away.

He took her in his arms and held her tight. "Wherever I go you go too," he said breathlessly in her ear.

"They will have speaker for you wherever they take you." She said struggling with tears.

He held her out at arms- length and looked at her with pleading eyes and tone. "Heck Shadow, I ain't troubled about no translators. I only know that I can't be right anymore without you by my side. I need you in my life. I don't really know why but some unknown power has brought me here." He pulled her close again and said tenderly, "you are part of what is happening to me." They held each other for several minutes before he added, "I love you Shadow."

Rubin was trying to figure out if his journey had reached the final destination. He was a thousand miles short of the distance the Lewis and Clark team covered. In the beginning of the trip he thought he would go all the way to the west coast and back. The only question he ever had, was how long it might take to ensure the right people heard about the troubled times they expected for the entire Indian nation.

As he and Joe journeyed along the river path, they spoke to leaders of all the tribes they stayed with. He didn't want to leave pursuing other clans for meetings that may or may not be as successful as this one was turning out to be. Besides, Shadow was here.

This posed a question of himself. Had being in love with Shadow changed his priorities? Should he allow this to happen? Should he allow love on any level to direct him elsewhere?

She was learning things being his interpreter. Subjects normally addressed by men. There was no offense of this design. She and most other women were focused on domestic development. This was the highest honor in their culture. Women owned all property. The children of the women stayed with her and her clan side. Men needed the approval of the Clan woman or the woman he was married to, before he could do much. This included going to war. Shadow's constantly expanding awareness of social and cultural problems, within her culture and beyond, motivated her to become more involved with solutions on a more extensive level. Her life had become more complicated. She sighed heavily.

Rubin became emotionally bound to her. And she had developed her own kind of bond to him. A special awareness of life and of themselves developed. Her passion for him and obligations to her community were hard to balance. She needed to talk to him intimately about many things but found it difficult because of the limitations imposed by her tribal customs.

He desired private time with her, too. He just wanted to sit with her and talk about anything that was just about them. But the *Wooesa* custom required him to wait until an elder of the village purposefully arranged for them to be alone.

Being patient was the best way, he grudgingly told himself. He believed he saw in Shadow's eyes a desire equal to his own. He wanted to set himself apart from other white men by allowing the customs of the tribe, to run its course. He was learning that compromising and surrendering had a mysterious way of giving back.

Deprivation was one of the many lessons the old Shaman spoke of, a lesson of life delivered through the normal course of living. People who wished to be guided by the spirits had an obligation to identify with these lessons and learn from them.

Hunger was another example of deprivation. For the Native American, hunger was common. Their hunger gave them reason to change their hunting grounds periodically. It also motivated them to be imaginative, resourceful and conservative. Their health benefited by this arrangement. These virtues developed within the soul by being hungry.

In the months Rubin spent with the *Wooesa*, he learned to observe and be patient. He saw in himself, traits he didn't desire. Thunder Horse commented on his undesirable qualities as a small piece of something larger. Without being offended, Rubin considered how and why he was the way he was. He wanted to replace some of his bad, often offensive behavior with something more intelligent, and wholesome. Many people had virtues he tried to emulate with little success. Thunder Horse said he was the way he was for a very special unknown reason. His confusion over his persona gave him anxieties.

"How am I to communicate with people and gain their confidence if I can't stop seeing humor in everything? He smiled as he thought of this and his new, temporary serious attitude.

He became aware of a natural process of need and acquisition. It was a lesson he tried to extract something beneficial from. Watching the process work with people fascinated him most. Animals fed when hungry, napped when tired, and surrendered when the situation was hopeless. People were far more complicated but why? He could clearly see how problems develop because the needs of people are not properly understood.

This, he believed, was the biggest difference between the white man's culture and the native's culture. The Indians were closer to the natural way of life. They saw and lived it every day. Rubin knew, from his own recent experiences, that natural attunement could be achieved over a relatively short period of time. The Indians had hundreds, if not thousands, of generations of natural attunement in their development. He could never reach their level, he thought.

Even with their heightened spirituality, their sharpened physical and mental qualities, Rubin saw a problem. They were vulnerable to the white man and his technology. If the Indian was to successfully defend himself and his land from the white man, he would have to be more like him, thus self-defeating himself. This didn't make sense. Something was missing.

It was hard for him to accept, but according to Burning Tree, this was the *Creator's* plan. Their lives and their history would stand as testimony to the effects of living with nature. That was good. But their lifestyle will be changed forever by the surge of the white man or from themselves.

The white man had a different motivation for existence. Acquisition and control are the dominant philosophies. Slavery, white male control in politics, denial of women to participate in politics, were only a few categories that defined the white man's unbalanced way of living.

Few people in the white culture considered the lifestyle they lived as detrimental to other cultures. They certainly couldn't see a future where one day, this carefully cultivated lifestyle of consumption would be detrimental to their very existence. Reasons were given, rules and laws were made as needed, and just as often changed to suit more current situations. Deception, lack of strong morals, and behavior seemingly void of ethics, appeared to be the white man's natural way of living. This would be costly in the long run.

The only real plan or strategy was to acquire all one could by whatever means possible. This economic strategy, based simply on greed, gave little consideration to anyone or anything else. It was important not to think of the possible depletion of resources. Just the very thought could retard the rapid economic growth so very crucial to the white man's ideals.

The native culture focused on the wise use of resources and the natural plan of life and death. That said, very simply, the weak will perish and the strong will survive. It was the Creator's law — the survival of the fittest — that prevailed everywhere in nature. It was not always pleasant to witness but nonetheless it was there to see if one only opened their eyes.

The Native Americans cherished the animals and plants they shared their existence with. They would never think about killing a buffalo or any other animal just for its skin or feathers, and, particularly, not for fun! The white man slaughtered entire herds of buffalo for their hides only. The Indians looked at life with reverence, in stark contrast to the white man's way.

Rubin worried quietly about the possibility of enslavement of these natural human beings. Everyone knew of the atrocities being played out in the slave trade of the West Indies and Africa. He knew these proud and defiant people would rather fight and die than be enslaved.

He also learned that in those export countries, native blacks bartered their freedom by selling their fellow countrymen. It was betrayal and treason of humanity at the highest level. Still the trade existed because the demand was there.

Rubin now had an improved view of life and living. He had a lot to share with leaders of other tribes and he knew he would also learn more. The council of the Chiefs, Shamans, and Sachems from the west was rumored to be forthcoming. The people of the village became excited with anticipation of the festive atmosphere that would soon be prominent.

Shadow walked slowly alongside Burning Tree. He walked with the aid of a staff. She patiently took her time with the old man. Rubin removed his hat respectfully at their approach. He gave a slight nod in greeting. Then he spoke in Sioux, "Greetings Old One. You honor me with your presence." His eyes turned to Shadow and a grin grew uncontrollably on his face. Her eyes sparkled with delight. Her smile alone made his blood heat up.

They couldn't break their staring, fixated on each other, nor could they stop their adolescence grinning. The old Shaman looked from one to the other knowing he stood in the presence of two young adults in love. He cleared his throat to get their attention.

When he succeeded in breaking their spell, he began to speak.

"The truth about life has always and will always be around us. It has a way of finding a pure soul to settle in." He paused for a moment looking up into the deep, cloudless, blue sky. He seemed to be searching for something he couldn't find, perhaps an eagle. Then he focused on something high up and smiled. He returned his attention to Rubin. There was a trace of humor in his eyes. He looked at Rubin and said, with long, drawn out words. "Then all will be revealed." Shadow's eyes widened as she translated.

"You must deprive yourself of food and water for two days before the winds of truth can find you and blow through you." Burning Tree turned and slowly walked away with his lovely escort at his side. The old man stopped to have a word with a man and woman who came up to him. Rubin saw Shadow look over her shoulder to see him watching her. She smiled at him and his heart flew like a bird.

The first day of fasting passed without much trouble but the second day started out bad. Rubin awoke terribly thirsty and desperately hungry. He was miserable.

"What I gotta fast for?" he complained. Shadow told him with annoyance and firmness, how important it was to follow the Shaman's directions with honor. She emphasized the word "honor."

"Mountain Wind will know at a glance if you are pure," She said. "You must ignore small unimportant things if you are to become aware." He put his hunger and thirst aside. He wanted to show her he was worthy and capable. He was uncomfortable but under control.

The atmosphere in the village was festive. Visitors from distant tribes had been flowing in for several days. It was believed that Mountain Wind had arrived, though no one could honestly say they had seen him. Feasting was going on at the community level. This made fasting for Rubin extra hard. He could smell roasting meat and wanted badly to be part of the merrymaking. It seemed so unfair to him. This is what he was good at. But fasting was required of him. Shadow admired him for showing self-control.

In the early morning darkness of the third day they came for him. Two warriors, painted like demons, complete with large animal teeth fastened to their faces, charged into his tipi, waking him with a start. They pulled him up on his feet and pushed him out of his tipi as he struggled to complete dressing.

These warriors had enough weapons on them to start, finish, and win a small war. Rubin was impressed. He tried to compliment them on their hideous attire but was being pushed along much too fast to allow for chatter of any sort. Prodded across the common area of the village, he noted all the people were up and watching him. All were deathly quiet. Shadow, also being escorted, came from the opposite direction and joined him. "I guess this is the way a person gets invited to a party," Rubin said, smiling at her. She was too nervous to smile.

They were pushed along to the medicine lodge just a short distance away, coming to a stop just outside the entrance.

"Maybe we can eat now," Rubin said, forgetting the need to stop his inappropriate humor. She hushed him.

CHAPTER TWENTY THREE

The door to the lodge was a flap of multi colored animal hide. It was held open by a savage-looking Indian brave. Rubin and Shadow were pushed through the door and into the dark interior. They were both temporarily disoriented by the darkness.

They stood by a wall partition that separated them from the main lodge and the crowd that waited unseen on the other side. Burning Tree handed Rubin a gourd cup and urged him to drink from it. He obeyed. Shadow dug her fingers nervously into his arm, the pain from her grip causing him to grimace. Other unseen people now manhandled them into position on the other side of the wall. Seven imposing figures sat cross-legged on the ground before a small but brightly burning fire.

The humor so common in Rubin had been stilled. A realization of the seriousness of the situation settled in on him. These people were ready to hear him speak about worldly changes. He became unsteady on his feet as nervous tremors shook him.

He struggled to control hyperventilating. His self-control was rapidly slipping away. He looked to Shadow for support, but she was transfixed by the sight of Mountain Wind. She had, like most people, heard of this legendary Shaman, but had never seen him, yet she recognized him immediately.

Two large ram horns curled along the sides of the Shaman's head, fitting so perfectly they seemed to have grown there. The great Shaman wore a fleece robe made from a large mountain goat, wooly and white as snow. Rubin was amazed at the sight of Mountain Wind. He appeared to be twice the size of the other men. The other great chiefs sat in equal numbers along both sides of him, draped in buffalo robes. Shaggy haired crowns, with protruding bison horns, graced their heads. Their faces were painted elaborately but differently from one another.

Peering from under the horns, Mountain Wind seemed to be looking straight through Rubin. His face was a perfect chiseled stone mask, void of expression. Rubin's heart pounded harder by the minute. Shadow held a crushing grip on his upper arm, squeezing it into numbness.

He took a deep breath and began to pray silently. "Please, Joe, be with me now. Speak through me, wisdom from the well of your soul."

Chiefs from the Cheyenne tribes and the Lasso Teton Sioux sat cross-legged with stiff backs. Shamans of the Hidatsa and Arapaho tribes sat in like manner. The Pawnee and Mandan were also represented. These were seven of the most prominent and powerful Chiefs and Shamans west of the Mississippi River. They wore their finest beaded and tasseled buckskins.

An old woman stepped from the darkness to sit by the fire, attending a crock placed nearby. She stirred then ladled a liquid from the crock into small ceramic cups, setting each aside carefully. Burning Tree appeared from the darkness, dancing rhythmically to the beat of a tom-tom droning from somewhere unseen. He chanted melodically. Then he threw something into the fire that made it burst momentarily into wild, towering flames.

In that instant of illumination, Rubin saw into the depths of the lodge, where at least a hundred other people stood watching from the quiet darkness. They too were painted and waited like zombies for a command.

Burning Tree motioned for Rubin and Shadow to sit before the council members, and then slowly backed away, out of sight. The old woman served the drinks she had ladled out. First she handed a cup to Mountain Wind, her eyes never meeting his as she served him with her head bowed. Then she served the other Chiefs and Shamans, bowing to each as she served.

Only after serving all the council members did she offer a cup to Rubin. Shadow remained un-served at his side. She relaxed her grip on his arm slightly. He flexed his fingers, appreciating the fresh circulation. Her widened dark eyes held reflections of the flickering fire light.

Burning Tree made several chants. He was somewhere close but out of sight. Those chants were immediately followed by a low reply from the chorus of unseen scores. The drinks were slowly but continuously sipped until gone. Rubin drank after a nudge from Shadow and a slight nod from one of the Shamans. He nearly gagged on the pungent brew. It was nearly too foul to swallow. It was almost as bad as the drink Burning Tree gave him seconds after his arrival.

A large ceremonial pipe was lite and after much pageantry, passed around. Each of the council members took their turn puffing and inhaling great volumes of smoke from the elaborately decorated pipe. They then exhaled unbelievably dense clouds toward the fire.

Faces took form in the exhaled smoke as it was illuminated by the flames. The faces in the smoke looked at Shadow and Rubin. They blinked their ghostly eyes then elongated into thin wisps and vanished. After each had smoked, the pipe was returned to Mountain Wind. He took one final inhalation, blowing the smoke across the fire at Rubin.

Shadow watched in fascination as the smoke turned into images of hands and arms. The smoky hands and fingers touched Rubin's face tenderly. They touched his nostrils and slipped into his head quickly via these ports. His eyes widened and his heart thundered as he allowed his body to be invaded by the ghostly figures in the smoke.

The old woman took the pipe from Mountain Wind and handed it to Rubin. She made no eye contact and seemed in a separate reality far from the activities going on. All eyes were upon Rubin. He puffed and inhaled. The smoke seared his lungs and made his eyes water. It took an exceptional effort to control the cough reflex as the spirit of the smoke battled within to take control. He would not allow himself to choke and cough, embarrassing himself before the huge assemblage and breaking the spell.

He immediately started sweating as his ears began to ring. After a few short minutes he began to feel like he was floating in the air. Distorted images filled his eyes. He shook his head vigorously trying to clear his vision.

Shadow's voice echoed, but was still remarkably clear. "You will now learn from Mountain Wind. He will teach you much about all things, and show you all you need to see." Her voice rang in his ears and tickled his brain.

Rubin tried to speak but could not control his voice. His tongue seemed loose and uncontrollable. He thought then panicked! "How will I be able to tell them what I came here to say?" He trembled and became overwhelmed with anxiety. Then a deep, kind, reassuring voice spoke to him.

"Our souls have but one voice when we are here." All the faces of the Sachems and Shamans appeared before his eyes in a veil of smoke. They all spoke with one voice but without moving their lips.

Rubin discovered he could hear and understand the councilmen, even though he could not speak their language. He couldn't even speak his own language. "They can hear and understand my thoughts," he said to himself. He tried to focus his thoughts, realizing the others were hearing him.

He began to doubt his sanity as he watched each smoky head turn into a fine thread and enter his nostrils and exit again. A gust of wind carried them into the heavens.

The unified voice called to him again. "You have been stripped of your mortal senses. You can only see, hear, and feel with your newborn soul."

He was flying and seeing things he had never seen before. He imagined he spread his unseen arms out like a bird and felt the wind rush by. He believed for a moment that he had become an eagle. He saw everything at the same time and understood everything!

Rubin saw a point of light and felt himself pulled towards it. It grew in size as he flew towards it at an incredible rate of speed, then it flashed as he entered the light. It filled him as he watched all questions disappear. He suddenly knew what life was all about, and he knew why he was here. It all made perfect sense now. One question remained, but before he could articulate it, it was answered. His question was, why me? The answer was, why not you. We are all the same in the eyes of our *Creator*. Choosing a messenger is a matter of where you are when the need arises. He was there, and so was the need. A continuum of this process is infinite.

At this point Rubin assigned himself another mission for his other life in the *Real World*. He was going to tell this story to all who would listen. He now knew why his personality was the way it is. He was the way he was so he could attract people. He was supposed to be that way so he could tell the story. He smiled a heavenly smile.

He was going to tell a story about how to forgive and get along better. This he would do by convincing people that forgiving is possible by believing that everything happens for a reason. There is *A Higher Power* that orchestrates life on an incomprehensible scale. Believing this and accepting other parts that are not understandable can make a person's life fill with joy.

At this point misunderstandings that are at the root of all problems become nonexistent. Exchanging and compromising become sought after endeavors, thus changing the world for the better. All this is possible by seeing with the eyes of the soul, all that the *Great Spirit* has placed before us to learn from. All we have to do is see.

Rubin realized that any person achieving a particular level of spiritual atonement can be one of *The Real People*, regardless of gender, age, race, or culture. But here, in his condition, void of body and ego, he could be completely modest and humble allowing himself a rare opportunity to learn at this level. He knew what his life mission now was.

Agreement was acknowledged by a nod from the heads of the Indian leaders, followed by an accelerated rush into the cosmos.

CHAPTER TWENTY FOUR

Rubin flew through and beyond the clouds. His senses were sharper than they had ever been in his life. He wondered if he had died and this was the journey into the afterlife. But the unified voices of the Shamans and Sachems spoke out loud proclaiming this was a journey to learn. He would return to the reality he knew.

He didn't know why, but he suddenly remembered things his mother told him as a young boy. Every word his mother spoke, he heard again. Everything he had ever said or done was relived, every memory recalled, no matter how small or insignificant. He traveled so fast he caught up to the images of past deeds done and the sounds of past words spoken.

All things he had ever said or done existed at the same time, forever. Nothing ever went away. He noticed other searching souls occasionally intersecting with his path on this cosmic flight. He considered he might have evolved and developed many different eyes and ears. This was easier for him to believe than it was for him to explain to himself. He accepted with blind faith what was happening. And acceptance was the crucial point of sanity salvation, a test of the strength of his soul. Had he chosen to rationalize what he was seeing and hearing, he would have gone permanently insane. The voices of multitudes of wise people spoke.

"The rule of our *Creator* can never be understood by mortals. Your decision to accept and believe allows the door of higher learning to open for you. You have chosen wisely."

All things that would happen in his life would happen for a good reason. All the suffering he would endure, all the pleasures he would enjoy. All things no matter how insignificant they seemed at the time were necessary for his life to be complete. *God's* instructions, encoded in his soul, required him to live naturally. If he and others followed these instructions, then everything that was supposed to happen would happen. And everything that was supposed to come his way and be a part of his life would come.

This flight through the cosmos was a temporary condition, yet an essential part of his development. No mortal could exist this way in everyday life. This was an encounter with *God, the Creator, Wankan Tanka*. A temporary introduction to convince him *God* existed and had a plan for his life. He was meant to follow the direction of God, the Creator. If a person lived according to the will of *God*, then all would be well for everyone and everything, regardless of the outcome, regardless of intentions or devices. Of course, I know this, he said to himself. I've always known, I just didn't allow myself to believe I knew.

All the events of his past and all the events he thought would be a part of his future played out before the eyes of his mind. He tried to understand why he had ever lacked confidence in himself. He knew anything that happened to him in the future would be totally understood, anticipated, or simply accepted. And he knew he was capable of clearly understanding everything. Quite a change in his life from the way he had been.

Rubin took time to focus on certain details that had been a part of his living experience. He wanted to go deeper into every aspect of every event. He needed to see the reason behind each particular event in the story of his life." Ma always said all things happen for a reason." He believed that every movement, every word spoken, and every deed done, was intended to be. He also believed that those few who could see this formula of nature, of *God's* will, were usually the most peaceful of all people. It became obvious that those who live closest to nature could see it best and understand it most. Civilization is a manmade blindfold. He spoke reverently, "Oh, *Wankan Tanka*, if only everyone could see this, the world would be perfect."

The laughter he heard was deafening. It came from the deepest corners of the universe. It came from inside his head. A voice said, "Perfection is imperfect. To be perfect is to have nothing in your life that is perfect. Such is *My* plan. Such is *My* will."

Rubin felt the truth and it humbled him to the point of tears. He cried harder than he had ever cried in his life. Knowing the truth brought tears that flowed like a waterfall. This momentary thought caused his soul to shape-shift into a river and waterfall. He had suddenly become a living, breathing body of water. With only the slightest amount of willpower, he slipped back in time and became the body of water that took his brother Joe.

"I can do this, I must do this! I am the river and I will save my brother!" From this new and unique perspective, he saw Joe struggling in the water. Acting as a river with human compassion, he tried desperately to save him. He willed the river, which he had turned into, to raise Joe and keep his head up and out of the water. Then there he was, Joe standing on the shore. He had just escaped drowning by a miracle. He smiled and waved as if he understood.

Rubin loved and missed his brother so much his soul cried out with despair. In his weeping he shifted back to himself, back to his current time. He felt the comforting arms of *God* wrap around him and speak tenderly in his ear. "Joe is where I want him. You have done good. All is well."

The sensation of wind could only be described as a universal flow blowing as he sailed on and through its current. He had never known this experience before, but still he understood what it was about. Every action has a reaction, and in turn, every reaction has an action. This symphony of cause and effect is endless. He knew what would happen at that instant, and what would happen next. Knowing this made everything more sensible, more reasonable. He learned that even the flutter from the wing of a butterfly will reverberate through the universe, forever!

The face of Mountain Wind appeared before him and spoke. "I will show you the answer to the question you want to ask." As he spoke, Rubin's eyes could see the picture the Shaman's words were painting.

"All things are as they should be." His voice thundered. Mountain Wind looked at Rubin as a father would look at his child. He commanded him to follow. Rubin was led to a place where the land was free of human existence. He watched as nature seemed to be moving in fast motion, trying to demonstrate the reason for its actions. He watched as cruelty and death played their vital roles in the entire plan of existence. He became aware that cruelty and injustice were a condition existing in his mind and in the minds of others like him. The way he felt about things did not mean that *God, Wankan Tanka*, felt the same way.

Cruelty, suffering and death were all vital ingredients in *the code of life*. "Without suffering, there would be no pleasure, and without death, there would be no life." Death itself, taught lessons to be learned. And the knowledge that life is temporary is intended to make people aware of the critical need to be peaceful and generous. Yet that can only happen when a person is sensitive. This is the key allowing each and every person to receive the most benefit from life. Living this way will perpetuate the evolution we must go through before we can take our place in the heavens.

Burning Tree was right again, there was no injustice to the inevitable ruin of the Indian nation. Rubin had only thought there was. Fair and unfair was only a matter of opinion and was different for everyone and everything.

Death of the body did not mean the death of the spirit. Thought was the spirit and the spirit would never die. It had always been and will forever be. It will, however, change form just as all things change and evolve. Rubin saw billions of plants growing, then becoming food for more plants to grow, on and on and on, without the spirit of the plant dying.

He then became aware of himself changing form. He had become one of the *Real People*. His skin, his hair, and his awareness had become as if he had been born one of the *Wooesa*.

"Am I to understand the spirit of the *Real People* will live on in the white man's body?"

His answer came to him like a cold mountain wind blowing through his soul.

"When a person becomes aware of life as it is supposed to be, then that person becomes one of the *Real People*." A *Real Person* can be any color, and can be a man or woman. We all become One, the same.

The sudden awareness that the *Real People* were never in danger comforted him. He had been focused on the body, and life was never about the body. It was about love and how love made life fertile. Life was all about the soul and its evolution.

All people who are peaceful and respectful of life will be considered a part of the *Real People*, no matter their gender or race, no matter where they are in the history of human existence. That is why people of peace have so few conflicts in their lives. Rubin laughed at the tickling sensation he had all over his body when he realized the truth of reality.

He could see Shadow and feel how strong she was. She carried such a heavy burden, yet she carried it well with such a deep sense of pride. He cried for her and felt shame for the way he had at one time considered her and all women. The gender to which he belonged had enslaved women all over the earth. He wept from shame at his egotistical male ignorance. He wanted that part of him to be gone.

Emotions and information surged through him faster than an avalanche. His nerves were on a sharp edge. Even his hair had feelings. Laughing, he embraced Shadow's spirit and continued to fly. He joined in her happiness and fell deeply in love with her. Their bodies became one. He saw the sun and flew toward it laughing all the while he enjoyed the warming rays. Then he began to get too hot. He tried to fly away but could not. He was getting too close to the sun. Mountain Wind laughed and flew away.

Rubin began to panic. "I'm burning!" he cried out.

Mountain Wind continued to laugh as he sailed away into the depths of the universe.

"I'm burning! I'm burning!" Rubin screamed! Shadow's face became superimposed over the face of the sun.

"All is well," she tried to reassure him.

"But I'm burning," he cried, thrashing about. "All is well, my man," she said. "All is well." Her face now blocked out the sun, saving him from the heat. She smiled as she dabbed at his forehead with a cool wet cloth. Rubin blinked and looked into her face.

She held his head in her lap. They were outside somewhere and the sun was high in the sky. Tears streamed from the corners of his eyes as he stared at her.

"All is well," she said. Her smile was the most endearing thing he had ever seen. His tears would not stop. Her sympathetic smile reassured him that all was well. He looked at her with a deep sense of love and respect. He was sure he was looking at an incarnation of *God*. She bent over and tenderly kissed him. She stared into his eyes, communicating love and devotion, soul to soul. He knew he would be her slave, her protector, and her devoted man forever.

The bits and pieces of memories from this experience took refuge in dark unknown places in his mind. They hid there as though hiding from the mundane thoughts of everyday living that tried but could not dilute the profound importance of their existence. The experience of his encounter with *God* would forever be there, waiting to be recalled, waiting for a time to be used.

CHAPTER TWENTY FIVE

"They would have to see this to believe it." Rubin spoke these words in a low tone, more to himself than to the others. The sight he beheld enthralled him.

Rubin, Shadow, and Burning Tree sat on their horses, gazing out over a sea of grass. "They would have to believe it before they could see it." Burning Tree's response was quick and accurate taking Rubin by surprise.

He thought about it for a time. Yes, he agreed, a person does, in fact, have to believe in something before they can see it.

As far as the eye could see, there was nothing but grass. It flowed like the waves on the ocean as the invisible wind moved the golden stalks. The knee-high grass created a rustling chorus sounding like angles singing praises to God.

The three of them came here to watch and wonder about nature and the power it held, much as other people do by going to the ocean's shore to watch the waves. It was all the same, people searching for peace by looking into the omnipotent face of nature.

They rode to the top of a rise of land — not a hill, not a plateau, but a long gradual rising — to better view the spectacle. The power of the view couldn't be appreciated at a lower level. Here, they could see farther than they could ride in a day. Burning Tree wanted them to feel the impact of the living ocean. Rubin had seen ocean waves, and this reminded him of that, although these waves were more tranquil, slower, and more peaceful.

He had seen fields of grass like these on the expedition with Lewis and Clark, but now, after all he had learned, it looked and felt different. He was now a believer.

He referred to white people when he said "they." They, he knew, would see something radically different. A landscape to be settled, mined, or developed in some way. They would see future profits.

"They would have to believe this, before they could see it," Burning Tree reiterated without solicitation. He, too, meant white people when he said "they." Rubin stood looking at him with questioning eyes. He had learned much these past few months and realized these people were wise, kind, and compassionate, and were, without a doubt, in touch with the *Creator*, *Wankan Tanka*. He felt as though he understood why they were as they were. Yet, even after his *God encounter*, he still struggled to accept that these people, so perfectly accustomed to the land and of creation, as doomed.

Since his spiritually expanding experience in the medicine lodge with Mountain Wind and the numerous Shamans, Rubin tended to look at life and everything in it differently. He felt he was now one of these people, a *Wooesa*. Not quite exactly like them. No real genetic connection, more of a spiritual one. But that was all that really counted, to them and to him. He didn't have the experience of living on and off the land as they had. But he was coming along. Shadow praised him for his accomplishments, his learning, and adjusting to the living conditions she considered normal. She looked at him a little differently these days, less infatuation, a little more respect and admiration.

Burning Tree took a deep breath before he spoke again. "Without the ability to see with the eyes of the soul, the person is deprived of the true sight that only this way of seeing provides. They will never be able see the secrets of life playing out before their own mortal eyes. Never will they be able to learn the lessons that *Wankan Tanka, The Creator,* intends them to see and learn." Burning Tree locked eyes with Rubin to add, "They will never see the truth or understand the reason for life, and of living."

Shadow was quick to dismount her horse and assist the Shaman in dismounting. They walked slowly away. Rubin delayed, being caught up in the power of the view. He ran to catch up. They walked a considerable distance before they stopped. Shadow stayed close by the Shamans side.

Rubin noticed a particular look in her eyes. She's feeling it too, he thought. The feeling coming over them gave lightness to the body and a tingling to the senses. They both giggled like little children at the sensation. Rubin stepped closer to her. Shadow touched his fingers delicately with hers as their eyes followed those of Burning Tree as they gazed over the endless sea of grass. Rubin closed his hand around hers. Their eyes did not meet. They didn't have to. A surge of pulsating energy electrified their senses.

After they took several minutes to gaze upon the land and allow themselves to feel the power and see the expanse, Burning Tree continued his oration.

"People must first be at peace with themselves. This is a very important step in the process of being able to see. Problems and troubles can blind a person. A person must have faith that *Wankan Tanka* has control and all things happen for a very good reason. Believing this will allow a person to have peace in their life. Then they may see the reality that is always before them. Only the eyes of a peaceful person can truly see." His words sounded heavy with sorrow.

Rubin's newly-expanded mind processed thoughts faster than he would have believed possible only a few weeks ago. He knew things without being told. The tone in Burning Tree's voice sounded sorrowful because he knew there weren't many people who had peaceful eyes that could truly see. Rubin's soul felt pain knowing the white culture, for the most part, was blind, unable to promote peace.

"Those who see through the eyes of a peaceful soul will see the plan of life *The Creator, Wankan Tanka* intends. A person with this vision will see that everything needed for a harmonious life is already here, working according to *His* great plan," Burning Tree said, adding a long deep sigh.

The Shaman continued, "But as long as people want to see something that is not there, they will continue to struggle to make things the way they want to see them. It has always been a struggle for each of us to see with the eyes of our souls instead of the eyes in our heads. This confusion of sight is responsible for the conflicts between those of us who can see and those who have no vision."

Burning Tree turned and faced the prairie. He raised his arms and began to chant softly. In only moments, the wind changed from a pleasant breeze to a powerful draft. The sea of grass whipped and rolled with the fury of the rising wind. Rubin held his hat in hand to keep it from blowing away. Burning Tree lowered his arms, ceased his chanting, and turned to stare at him. The wind calmed almost instantly. Shadow's grip on his hand eased.

Rubin stood staring into the old Shaman's eyes. He felt he finally understood what it meant to be a real human, in touch with *God*, in touch with the land, in touch with himself, a true native of *Maka*.

CHAPTER TWENTY SIX

Rubin felt as though he had finally arrived at the perfect place and time. He was sitting on the ground with his legs stretched out in front of him. Shadow was close to him. Very close. She too, had her legs stretched in front of her. Her legs were covered with a supple, bleached, animal skin. He looked at her with adoring eyes and could not imagine a more perfect vision of beauty.

She had become comfortable with the way he quietly communicated affection toward her and didn't mind the way he stared at her for long periods without speaking. She, too, looked at him with adoration. Other adult village members had been around them earlier but they now purposely left them alone.

Rubin knew this was his opportunity, approved by the village elders. The fire burned close to their feet, warming them, creating a cozy, intimate atmosphere and giving off a wonderful aroma of hickory. The smoke from the fire was unobtrusive for a change. And where were all the noisy young people today? Rubin looked around suspiciously, expecting some sort of interruption. There was nothing! Even the barking dogs were far off in the distance. He smiled at Shadow with a nervous yet confident smile. "This is the time I've been waiting for," he said softly. She smiled expectantly. He moved closer.

A large log was a backrest and served as a bench for people at other times. Today it acted as a shield and it was all theirs. He scooted a little closer. Her smile grew even bigger as he stretched his arm out and nonchalantly let it close around her shoulders. He could smell her clean scent of wild mint and maybe, just a hint of lilac. As he sniffed around her throat, she began to pant softly. Her eyes implored him to come closer, so he did! Their eyes locked as their excitement grew.

"Shadow —" He gulped for air before he could continue. "— I've been waiting for a long time to have a talk with you, to be with you like this." She could tell he was nervous. That amused her. She began to giggle.

Rubin remembered a time, not too long ago when he asked Gus about the mysteries of women. Rubin thought Gus knew everything about women because he was married. Gus told him, in jest, that a giggling girl was ready to be kissed.

He went for it! Their lips tenderly touched as if they were speaking to each other mouth-to-mouth. Her mouth opened and she was about to commit herself totally. Then . . .

"Shadow, Shadow!" The voice rang out from the other side of the log. They nervously separated. A young brave leaped over the log and excitedly exclaimed, in their language, something Rubin didn't completely understand. She looked surprised but spoke to the young man calmly, in their native language. As they conversed, she became more and more excited.

"Francois." She spoke the name reverently. The young brave nodded his head with excitement. Shadow was now ecstatic. She jumped to her feet and ran away shouting, "François," over and over as she disappeared.

Rubin slumped down feeling totally dejected. "I'll be damned," he said to no one in particular. He jammed his hat down hard on his head.

It looked like the entire village had focused on, and now ran to see this one special person. They stampeded as though they would receive a divine blessing. Rubin tried desperately to find out what was going on and who the person was. He was told only, "Francois!" Happy faces rushed by him as though he didn't exist. Slowly he made his way to where the group gathered.

The crowd pressed together tightly. Rubin couldn't see anything. Dogs barked and ran about as though intoxicated by the excitement of the people. Everyone chattered at the same time. Hysteria seemed to reign supreme. A large tree standing close to the crowd's edge gave Rubin an idea. With a little difficulty, he managed to climb up and perch himself on a branch. Finally he could see.

The stranger strode among the villagers slowly with a step and posture that emanated strength and confidence. He was much taller than anyone in the village. Long silver hair, combed back over his head, hung down to his shoulders. Silver stubble covered a face seemingly chiseled from stone. He wore a very clean white blouse, open almost to his navel. Silver hair covered his muscular chest. He smiled as he walked, greeted everyone and seemed to know everyone's name.

Rubin spotted Burning Tree approaching the man to extend his hand in greeting. Rubin stared with disbelief. Burning Tree was smiling! "I don't believe it!" he exclaimed out loud, not being able to contain his astonishment, but no one heard him. He had never seen Burning Tree smile.

Then everyone stopped moving and talking at the same time. The silver-haired man struck a pose with his hands on his hips and his feet spread shoulder's-width apart. He motioned with one hand for someone in the crowd to come forward. It was Shadow!

She held her hands together and close to her bosom as if she were praying. She took tiny steps as she walked up to this magnificent-looking man. The smile on his face grew as he took her in his arms. He had turned so Rubin could not see anything but his back. But he thought he saw this man raise Shadow's chin with one hand and bend down to kiss her.

"No!" Rubin screamed! He lost his balance and fell from the tree.

He lay on his back, nearly knocked out. It took him several minutes before he recovered enough to realize he had just made a fool of himself in front of someone very important to the tribe. His eyes fluttered open. The silver-haired man looked down on him.

"Are you okay, my friend?" He spoke French and Rubin had no clue what he said. They studied each other intensely. Rubin blinked to focus. He turned his head to one side to see Shadow looking at him with interest and concern. He could not hide the hurt he felt inside. He looked at her as if to say, "Good-bye, my love." It had ended before it got started. Shadow picked up on that immediately. She drew back as if she had just uncovered a snake. Alarm showed in her eyes.

"I've never seen you before," the silver-haired man continued. He looked to Shadow and addressed her. "Do you know this man?" Shadow nodded her head in confirmation. Rubin knew she could speak French but he never put it all together, until now. He looked down at Rubin. "I am Francois, Francois Johnette Lafayette." Rubin's brow furrowed with confusion. "I don't know what you're saying, mister." He looked at Shadow and smiled. His smile came from a man with a broken heart. "Hey there Shadow," he said. They both gave each other long looks. Her expression revealed confusion. He turned his attention to the long- haired man. "I don't what you're saying but, howdy, anyway."

"Forgive me, sir." The man switched his speech to English. "Here, let me help you up." He extended his hand to Rubin. "My name is Francois, Francois Johnette Lafayette, at your service sir."

"That's better, now I can understand you," Rubin answered. He straightened up to be as tall as he could possibly make himself, yet Francois was still at least a head taller. "My name is Rubin." He cleared his throat and began again. "My name is Rubin Winslow Field, and I'm at your service, sir." They shook hands but looked at each other cautiously.

Francois raised a hand to his chin in thought. He took in all the emotions reflecting in Rubin and Shadow's faces. Forlorn loss showed on Rubin's face. Shadow's eyes were filled with confusion. Francois contemplated the situation during the awkward silence. A single eyebrow rose as he looked from Shadow to Rubin, then back to Shadow. His beaming smile revealed his understanding.

"Let's take a walk and have a smoke," Francois said smiling at Rubin. This was a universal man code meaning they had to talk in private. Rubin nodded in agreement. Francois addressed Shadow, saying they would rejoin her later.

As they were leaving the village they walked by the small tipi Rubin called home. All his belongings were there. "Mind if I grab my Springfield?" It was a rhetorical question. He grabbed it as they walked by.

"I've been having some problems with this thing since it took a drink." Francois didn't quite know what to think, but felt no danger despite what he knew was a misunderstanding in Rubin's mind.

"What's been the problem with it, my good fellow?"

"I can't get the danged thing to fire," he retorted.

CHAPTER TWENTY SEVEN

They walked for a long time in total silence. Francois had a troubled, uneasy expression on his face and kept looking over his shoulder. His behavior and suspicion became contagious. Rubin felt it now and looked around vigilantly also. They both believed they were being followed, but nothing could be seen among the short grass spreading out in every direction, offering little cover.

Despite his uneasy feeling, all Rubin could think of was this man holding and kissing the woman he loved. He felt empty, stripped of everything he wanted and held dear. The steps he took became more and more laborious.

With every step and every glance at Francois, he asked himself who he thought he was to expect Shadow to really love him. If he and Francois walked all day long and went nowhere, he wouldn't have cared. He slowed several times, feeling ready to lie down and stare at the sky. This emotional drain left him exhausted. They finally came to a place far from anyone or anything. Francois stopped abruptly.

"Let me explain myself, please." That opening statement startled Rubin. He jerked to full attention. "I've waited a long time to see this." Rubin looked at him totally confused. What could this man be talking about he thought?

"What I see is love, my good fellow," Francois said earnestly. "I see Shadow in love," he continued.

Rubin stepped back as if struck. Of all the things he expected from Francois, this wasn't one of them.

Francois studied Rubin, and then added," She's in love with you, Mister Rubin. And you are the one she's been waiting so long for." Francois gave him a fatherly smile.

Rubin looked confused and irritated at the same time. Then he sternly asked, "If she loves me, and you know it, why did you hold and kiss her?"

Francois burst into uncontrollable laughter. When he could finally speak, he said, "Please forgive and believe me, Mister Rubin, but I hold and kiss my dearest Shadow as I hold and kiss my daughters." Francois shook his head amused and disbelieving Rubin's assumptions.

"Forgive me, sir, but I am a Frenchman and it is my habit to kiss and love women." He shrugged his shoulders as a sign of confession, surrendering to his habits. Then Francois said with a serious tone, "Though Shadow is a young attractive woman, I am old enough to be her father."

Rubin regarded this perspective with skepticism. Then slowly he began to smile. As his smile grew, Francois gestured to him with an, "Ah, now you've got it," expression. They both laughed hard. Rubin's world was a much better place once more.

Filled again with happiness and hope, he recognized his quick moods swings were caused by love. Now he was eager to return to the village, to see Shadow, to hold her in his arms, and to tell her how he felt about her.

"Feeling better my friend?" Francois asked with genuine concern.

Rubin smiled and nodded. The man has got way too much height and hair, he thought. His smile is way too big and his shoulders way too broad. He looked Francois over and saw the man he wished he could be. He could easily dislike him — and had! —but how quickly that dislike had changed! "Yes sir, I feel just great, thanks."

Francois slapped Rubin on the shoulder. It nearly knocked him over and it definitely hurt, but Rubin wouldn't let him know that.

"Let us look at your gun," Francois said, grinning. It was one of those things men do when they want to share time together, fidgeting with mechanical things or solving problems. They examined the gun in minute detail.

"It seems to be all right," Francois said. They prepared it for firing. "Have a go of it, sir."

He handed the weapon to Rubin. He raised the Springfield to his shoulder and aimed at the horizon and pulled the trigger. A puff of smoke, accompanied by a simultaneous, impudent fizzle from the flash pan was all the normally powerful Springfield produced. Rubin sighed. Francois looked confused as he scratched his chin.

Not too far away Shadow crawled closer, still unobserved. She could not hear them but she could read faces very well and was pleased they were getting along and not fighting. She licked her lips, anticipating kisses she desperately wanted from Rubin. Not a kiss like the one on the forehead from the silver-haired, father figure. She had known Francois since childhood. He was the man who taught her and other villagers French. She was curious about communication with the frontier people, so he taught her English too. He said both would be very helpful to her in the future.

He was a mountain man who usually passed through twice a year, once on the way out and once on the way back to his home and to his wife and daughters. Shadow knew all this. She knew Rubin would feel better about Francois once he learned how kind and generous he was. And she knew how much better he was going to feel when she would kiss him and tell him how much she loved and wanted him.

She just began to crawl away, feeling she had seen enough and not wanting to be discovered. Then she heard a snake's rattle. She bit her lip in aggravation. "Not this, not now!" she thought. Turning her head slowly from one side to the other, she located the rattling serpent, coiled and ready to strike.

She quickly rolled to one side. At the motion, the snake struck, barely missing her. The snake pulled back into its coil as she jumped to her feet and backed away. The snake had forced her to reveal herself.

Rubin and Francois were visibly stunned at her presence. Francois looked at Rubin, who was looking at Shadow, who was looking back at them, and they all had looks of disbelief written on their faces. She only looked desperate for a moment, and then quickly said, "I've been looking for a wandering child." She searched their faces to see if they were buying her excuse. "Have you seen a child anywhere?"

Francois began to smile. "Mister Rubin, you are going to have yourself a wonderful woman — " He paused to look back at Shadow standing just a few yards away, trying not to look too embarrassed. Then he looked back to Rubin, "If you can handle her."

CHAPTER TWENTY EIGHT

Francois asked, "Tell me a little about yourself. It seems everybody here knows you."

Rubin looked about as if to confide with a multitude of people, but they were alone.

They told Shadow she would do better with her search if she headed back to the village. A child would hear the sounds of the village or smell fires and cooking food and knew enough to go to those sounds and scents. The lie she told them and the lie they told her were of equal benefit and satisfaction. She nodded her head rapidly in agreement and left them, heading toward the village.

"I have two other brothers and we have land where the three rivers join. My brother Joe and I came from St. Louise to bring a message to the Indians." He hung his head and said, "I lost Joe in the river a month ago."

"I am so sorry you lost your brother. I've lost two brothers." Francois said with a deep sigh. They both stood silently for a minute while they sorted their emotions.

Francois shook himself free from his painful thoughts first and commented on the homestead Rubin referred to. "I thought a French family lived there. I remember a farm, with a house and a barn, and a small Indian village close to the banks of the river."

Rubin shrugged his shoulders. "They were bought out by the government. We own it now."

He asked, "Where in France are you from and why are you here?"

He made himself comfortable anticipating a long answer. He stretched out on his backside, lacing his hands behind his head.

Francois sat down on a log. "I'll tell you something that might make you think poorly of me." Rubin sat up, looking more interested.

"My native country is France. I was born and grew up in a little town called Vernalis, a little place just a few miles north of Paris. I became the proud mayor of Vernalis; at least I was proud for a short time. As mayor I traveled to many cities to study and share ideas with other mayors about social situations and how to make things better. I quickly learned things about people I wish I had not. I learned that people where I lived were not strong and could be easily manipulated."

"I saw too much fighting, lying, and cheating. I was ashamed of my country, my town, and the people I was elected to serve. Forgiving them for their behavior was more than I was capable of. I couldn't understand why they behaved the way they did." He shuffled his feet like a boy ashamed of himself. "The issue that made me leave was finding out our national government was planning to deliberately deceive and use people for their selfish gain!" Rubin stiffened, recognizing the similarity in his own situation.

"So I left my home and country to seek out a land where people were of better," he thought for a long time once again before saying, "better spiritual quality."

In a tone that said his words were of little or no importance, he added, "I found passage on a merchant ship, working as a deck hand to pay my fare to come to this land. I heard from other travelers and explorers that this foreign land, under French rule, was more proper for an idealist like myself. I arrived here some fifteen years ago. I found a beautiful, loving Shoshone woman and married her. We have two daughters. I travel back and forth from Cincinnati,

Ohio, to the land of the Mandan just a week or so north of here." He looked at Rubin as if asking if he knew where the Mandan lived.

Rubin chewed on a piece of twig. "You obviously haven't heard. This land no longer belongs to France. That's how my brothers and I acquired our land. This land is part of America now and has been since a General named Napoleon sold it to our president, Mister Thomas Jefferson."

Francois raised his hand to his chin. Rubin's steadfast stare left little doubt in the mind of Francois that Rubin spoke the truth. It took several minutes before Francois could speak. "When?"

Rubin stood up. "Not long ago, maybe four years or so. The way I heard it, Mister Napoleon needed some money to finance another military campaign so President Jefferson handed him fifteen million dollars and said thank you very much." Francois shook his head slowly, and then started to laugh. In a few seconds Rubin was laughing, too.

Francois sat down again. "There was talk of it before I left home, but I guess I never believed it would happen. I guess their greed just caught up with them, but my France . . . It's just hard to believe they'd be that stupid."

They spent the afternoon talking about politics, religion, and exploring, and actually began to accept and like each other. Francois was as familiar with Europe as any man could be. They talked about and compared the differences between the philosophies of the Native Americans, Europeans, and the Americans.

Rubin took extra care communicating to Francois, the prophecy of Burning Tree. "He said the destiny of humanity was," he pointed and looked up at the same time.

Francois looked up, then back down. He pointed upward and asked, incredulously, "In the sky?!"

Rubin answered factually, "More precisely, in the stars," Francois looked flabbergasted. "Burning Tree believes Indians are supposed to suffer and die so we white people can learn from their misery." He finished his statement with a look of skepticism.

"Learn what?" Francois asked bewildered.

"Burning Tree says we have to destroy the Indian nation so we can learn what not to do when we go exploring up there. He says we got to learn what not to do to the," he thought for a moment before he spoke. Then he slowly said, "The Indians up there, I guess!"

Francois stood up again, standing in a pose Rubin took as that of an educated thinking man. "What do you think of his prophecy, Mr. Rubin?"

Rubin's eyes burned with intensity as he carefully considered his answer. "I know something about exploring, Mr. France." Francois took a step back, startled. "I went with Lewis and Clark all the way to the Pacific Ocean and back. I learned white people came out here to see what could be taken advantage of. There is little or no regard for these people and their way of life, and there will be even less of it in the future." He threw down the twig he'd been chewing on as if disgusted with it.

"I don't doubt that someday there will be explorers that go to other places," he went on, looking up and shaking his head. "I don't know how anybody or anything can get," he waved his hands despairingly at the sky. "Up there anywhere, but —" Both men fell silent in thought. Then Rubin concluded. "I've seen a billion stars with the eyes in my head, and I've traveled to places with my soul. I am convinced there are other places and, no doubt, other native cultures to be discovered when the time is right."

Francois listened, clearly impressed with Rubin's perspective. Not much existed in the way of facts or science to support his thoughts of excursions into the depths of space. But there was a feeling deep inside each man telling them there was something else beyond what they now believe as real. And somehow, ways would be found to do something as spectacular as crossing an unknown land, unknown water, or space of any kind. They would explore unknown lands, make contact, and declare peace at all cost. They could then exchange knowledge and resources to improve the lives of all cultures.

This will be a reoccurring event throughout the history of man. Wonderment and dreams spawn exploration. As it was with prehistoric explorers rafting along an uncharted river, as it was with Lewis and Clark, as it will be for all explorers in the future.

Without any way of knowing for sure, they were both convinced something else existed far away, other inhabitants different from us, yet of the same spirit. They believed in life.

CHAPTER TWENTY NINE

Francois resumed his journey back to Ohio a week earlier. He was instrumental in setting so many things right. Rubin bonded well with him. As a promise, they agreed to seek each other out in the future to share and compare their insights on life, love and family. It was because of Francois that Rubin would be able to talk about life that was again filled with the joy of love and hope.

Today he stood with Shadow and Burning Tree. They were near the edge of a high bluff, feeling as though they were at the center of a vast emptiness.

The sound resonating from the bluff held an earthly tone, nearly silent. If a person tried hard to hear, the tone faded away. If they relaxed, they could hear the earth breath. That soft sound was broken only by the sighs of gentle breezes rustling the sparse grasses. Mild moans and quiet whistles struggled to reach the ear. Rubin looked around and wondered if an invisible life force was searching for recognition.

As a breeze manifests its true form in otherwise shapeless smoke, the power of life manifested its true form in the three free spirits standing atop the bluff. They were transfixed by a peaceful, calm feeling. The undeniable strength of the blissful void filled Rubin with tranquility and silent power.

He wondered about the origin of the strength that seemed to surge through him as he willed himself, by the direction of Burning Tree, to empty himself of aspirations. 'It's odd,' he thought, "I expose myself to the basic elements, and I become perfectly peaceful and content. I want for nothing and get everything."

For a slight moment he wondered if these feelings of contentment could be a deception of sorts. It only took one quick look at Shadow to convince him that this way of life was right for him and deception did not thrive here. He saw her, standing before him. A beautiful, healthy, young woman, she took nothing and gave everything.

Rubin stepped back to get a better look at her, all of her. She was as fit and alert as any person could be. Her lifestyle had created and shaped her. Hard work, natural food, and clean air were all we were intended to have, by decree of *God, The Great Spirit, Wankan Tanka.* His observation of her and his spiritual rational ended.

Shadow, too, looked out into the vast emptiness. Her life and soul firmly bonded with Maka.

He asked Burning Tree. "Is it true the land and the spirit living here make us what we are?"

Burning Tree responded with sign language and a few words. "Land and spirit are one." He gestured, by waving his hand over the land. "We are one with all."

Rubin rephrased his question. "Does the spirit of the land make people think and act the way they do?"

"*Maka,* and *The Great Spirit,* do not blind or deafen people," Burning Tree answered.

"Can I make a difference on the land, or does the land make a difference on me?" Rubin asked as a final attempt of an answer. Burning Tree quietly studied Rubin after the translation.

He waved his hand across the vista. "What do you see?"

Before Rubin could answer Burning Tree said, "Do you not see mountains that have been worn down to sand? Can the eyes of your soul not see the power the mountain once held? The mountain was once too high to walk over. People walked around because the mountain had the power. Now we walk on it.

You must realize the answers to your questions change as the mountain crumbles. Our lifetimes are more than the stars in the heavens before the mountain becomes a vast emptiness. Can you allow yourself to feel the power of the mountain?" Burning Tree waved his hand at the view before them. Rubin felt like he saw the mountain.

Then the answer to his question formulated in his head. Nature has a power to change and manifest in a multitude of forms. Understanding the time it takes for the power to change form is what now lay at his feet, sands of time. He saw the changes in everything that surrounded him and knew everything was created for a reason and a time for its existence. The truth of nature is undeniable, *the code of life* governing every creature and life form on earth.

The temporary confusion Rubin experienced was quickly made clear. He had to remind himself the reality of life as it was evolving. It is often misunderstood as an out-of-control problem. Yet, in fact, it is an orderly process. If learned and lived properly, it promoted growth of body and soul.

The old Shaman watched Rubin ponder the meaning of these new thoughts, this new reality.

Burning Tree said little more. It was time for Rubin to test his newly evolved sight.

"We must leave you," Burning Tree said softly.

"I must stay," Rubin responded with determination. He knew something profound was close and he swelled with confidence wanting the encounter.

Burning Tree understood. The old Shaman turned to leave. Shadow took the old man's arm to slowly escort him away. As she left, she gave Rubin a knowing look. She knew he had to be at peace in his own mind before he could be at peace with anything else. He watched them for several minutes until they were out of sight.

He turned his attention back to the vast emptiness. He closed his eyes and took in a deep breath. He felt a soft breeze swirl around him. Like an embrace from a lover, the warm breeze enclosed him, caressing his face like a kiss. The soft, rustling sounds the breeze made came to him, like a woman whispering. He trembled, looking about nervously then shouting out loud, "Are you *God?* Are you with me now?" The strength of the breeze rose. A sudden gust of warm air pushed him back a step. Then everything became absolutely still.

The atmosphere became so still he thought he heard a soft ringing. It was a sound heard not by mortal ears but only by the inner ear of the soul. A strange feeling similar to that of free falling almost set him off balance. He masterfully maintained his balance and beamed inwardly knowing he had gained control.

He sat down at the edge of the bluff, a cliff falling away beneath his feet, starring out into the vast emptiness. He stood for hours, watching as the sun slowly set over the horizon and the procession of day time life slowed itself to a stop. One by one, stars filled the night sky until it seemed billions of them twinkled and sparkled overhead. He felt the depth of all creation. He sat for many more hours, watching everything with eyes and ears that could now truly see and hear.

CHAPTER THIRTY

"Where's Rainier? I need his help," Rachel told Gus impatiently. "Let me help you," he said.

She stared at him for a long moment. She seemed perturbed. "Okay," she said. "Pluck those chicken carcasses over there and sort the feathers for our pillows and mattresses. You do know how to separate down feathers from quilled, don't you?" she asked with a dreadful glare. "And after you're through with those . . ."

"I'll find Rainier," Gus interrupted. He knew she would keep adding items until he gave up.

He should have known by the way she asked for Rainier that only he would do. He walked from the house smarting from the knowing glare she gave him.

She created special chores for Rainier, doing so just so she could have someone other than him, her husband, to talk to. She desperately needed a confidant. And she knew everything she said to Rainier would be kept in confidence.

Rachel was a woman badly needing another woman around, a friend, neighbor, and collaborator. But she had none. No sister, mother, no best friend. Rainier was the next best thing and, sometimes, Gus felt sorry for both of them. He knew Rainier sat and listened to long hours of chatter, and doing meaningless chores just so Rachel would have him close by to listen to her. He imagined there were probably times of meaningless crying and emotional ups and downs also. The more he thought about it, the worse he felt for both of them.

Gus felt no threat by the special intimacy his wife shared with Rainier. He knew the problem, and wished he knew how to save Rainier from the domestic situation, but he felt he might be punishing Rachel by doing so.

"Things will be different when the baby comes," He told himself.

But what a dilemma. Without a better solution, he had to let things be as they were. He felt especially indebted to Rainier for all the extra work he did for Rachel. It was not a part of the initial work agreement. Reluctantly he set out to find him.

"There you are." Gus sighed deeply, relieved to find him standing by the corner of the barn looking out toward the east. He walked up and put his hand on his shoulder. He was just about to speak when the words froze in his mouth. His eyes followed the path of Rainier's steadfast gaze. Now he stood staring with him.

What had been out of sight from the house was now in clear view. A small group of apprehensive-looking Indians approached from the river village, leading a horse and carrying baskets and ropes. Gus counted three women and four men.

"I thinks we be gonna have company fo dinna," Rainier said softly over his shoulder, not moving.

Greetings were made in sign language. The men had a group smoke after introductions. Nervous smiles and shuffling feet amused Gus. He didn't want to offend or frighten them so he proceeded cautiously with his words and movements.

The women stood close by with smiles intact, watching the men smoke. Gus was deliberately slow in calling Rachel out for introductions.

The Indian women felt at ease after seeing the men at peace with each other. They walked to the corner of the barn and pointed toward the house, asking unintelligible questions. Rachel soon appeared at the door and was as apprehensive as the Indian women had been initially.

The Indian women slowly approached her, smiling, extending their baskets and chattering all the while. A bemused Rachel could only nod and offer a confused greeting to them. The ladies scampered into the house with Rachel.

Rainier was presented with a great looking black horse on a tether. He was astounded at the gift. The Indians were curious, wanting a closer look at his skin and hair. They were amazed, as most Indians were at the sight of a black man. They had to touch and examine. Rainier played the good sport and allowed them to satisfy their curiosity. He seemed honored.

The group presented Gus with a braided rope, a knife and a tomahawk. He was also lectured about what he thought was something about the river or the pasture or the cattle, or maybe it was about Rachel, he couldn't tell. The pipe they had smoked was also given to Gus, along with a pouch of herbs. The smoke from the herbs was mild, pleasant, and gave Gus a mellow, euphoric feeling. He appreciated that very much.

The Indian men seemed surprised, and very happy, when Gus pointed to several cattle and made gestures to show he was giving the cattle to them. Now the tension had been completely dissolved. Gus pointed toward the house and made a motion for them to follow him.

Rachel was ecstatic to meet other women. It didn't matter who they were or that they didn't understand what each other said. The kind intent from both groups was clearly understood. And even though they didn't understand each other's language, they understood each other, nonetheless.

The men sat, smoked, and drank coffee, eating sweet bread Rachel served along with berries and slices of squash the Indian women brought. They quickly taught Rachel a new recipe. They called it *"wojapi."* They whipped it up in a hurry right there so Rachel could watch and learn. It turned out to be a very simple, and very good fruit pudding. All the time they talked and gestured, the Indian women gently touched Rachel's enormous belly. Even with the language barrier, the Indian women made it clear they intended to help Rachel with her delivery.

The women held hands firmly, bonding. The anxiety Rachel had harbored disappeared completely. Tears welled in her eyes as she tried desperately to tell these new friends how happy they made her. The tears and smiles spoke volumes for all.

Gus surmised from what the men were trying to tell him that Yumni had taken a detour and dropped in on friendly, fellow tribesmen. Yumni had not only brought Gus and Rachel great news about Rubin and Joseph, but had set into motion an event that finally brought neighbors together. Gus made a promise to himself to find Yumni someday and thank him for all he had done.

Later, as Gus, Rachel, and Rainier escorted their neighbors to the fence by the barn to say goodbye, they tried to make it understood they would visit them in their village very soon. They all felt a new happiness knowing they had good, peaceful neighbors just a short ride away.

CHAPTER THIRTY ONE

They had been sitting cross-legged, side by side for hours, watching the night sky as if they were searching for something. Stars shimmered and glistened. An occasional streak of light redirected their attention, but only for the shortest time.

Rubin's acclimation into the world and lifestyle of this tribe over the past several months had led him to this time and place. He not only felt he belonged with the native people, he lived as one. The person he had been several months ago no longer existed. Even the life changing experiences during the Lewis and Clark expedition didn't compare to the total life change he had undergone while living with the Wooesa. His transformation was nearly complete.

The fire they lit cast a soft light and radiated warmth. Coyotes called to each other, their distant mournful cries drifting through the night air, adding an ambient song to the mystical atmosphere.

Rubin was filled with wonder. His newfound understanding of life redefined everything. All commonplace sights and sounds now inspired new feelings deep within his soul.

His attention turned to Shadow. She too, was mesmerized by the fantastic view of the night sky. She shivered. He reached for her. The soft touch of her doe skin shirt aroused him. He could feel her slight shoulders under her garments. Turning her face toward him, she smiled with a catlike look in her eyes. She was soft, fragrant, and feminine. The natural woman in her called silently to the natural man in him. He could smell her womanly scent.

She brought the fire in him to full flame. His mouth watered. He had an uncontrollable urge to taste her. They leaned together in a kiss. Her lips were soft, warm and sweet. He held her close and tight.

Her eyes spoke silent imploring words. They were saying, "Take me. I'm yours." With one arm around her, he held her as though she were his captive. This aroused her. Her breath quickened. He tilted her head. Like a hungry animal, his open mouth covered hers. She was ready and waiting for him. Their tongues flicked and explored. She too, was hungry for love.

He gently, but firmly, eased her back. She was eager and didn't resist. He took only a small moment to straighten the elk skin they had brought to lay on. He had to know she was comfortable before he could go any farther.

"Are you okay?" he asked in a deep, husky voice. She couldn't speak but nodded her head. His hands explored her tender, womanly treasures. He struggled to control his lust. She encouraged him to go farther by spreading her legs. He laid himself carefully on top of her. As they kissed, she writhed in sensual ecstasy under him. Her hips raised and ground against his pelvis. He knew this was the time.

Clumsily, he pushed himself free from her to strip. The chilly, night air nipped at his skin, arousing him further. With a quick hand she pulled a few ties loose and removed her leggings and skirt. He looked with amazement at this beautiful woman.

The sight of her sitting naked on her folded legs looking up at him aroused him so much it was painful. Her skin was smooth, tight and brown. Her vibrant soft curves demanded his hard muscles to make her complete. She ran her hands slowly over her breasts and down her waist to her pelvic mound. She squeezed her legs together as if trying to crush her hands. This movement pushed her breast together. She was unaware of the sensual show she was putting on for him. He became an enchanted captive, unable to speak

He lay atop her with his incredibly hard manhood pressing down on her. She took him in her hand, squeezing and pulling on him. He moaned with pleasure he had never known before. She pulled her legs up, guiding him toward her womanhood. Her body swallowed him. His moan of pleasure echoed throughout the valley. She quivered and moaned beneath him. Her legs wrapped around his waist tightly, except to spread and push against the ground raising him up. The wild animal in her had been released and he had freed it. He held her hands down above her head with one of his hands. She loved the feeling of being held down. Pushing against the ground and grinding in loving, passionate acceptance.

She rocked her hips, allowing him to penetrate deeper. His mounting pleasure was growing uncontrollably. They spent more than an hour bound as one. Their lips were becoming sore and tender from so much kissing. He was unaware of anything except loving her. He had become lost in time. She clawed at his back with her finger nails and began a grinding movement that allowed him to penetrate deeper. This brought him to his climax. He covered her mouth passionately with his as he screamed with pleasure and exploded inside her. He licked and nibbled on her lip as he panted. She arched her back as she convulsed. She took one deep, gasping breath after another. Rubin could feel and hear her heartbeat. They were both breathing like race horses at the finish line.

Their hearts beat madly. Their eyes spoke of love too deep for words. They melted into each other's loving embrace, reaching a state of total bliss. Several minutes passed before he, with difficulty, rolled to his side and sat up holding her still impaled on him. He held and controlled her limp, spent body in his lap. He repositioned his legs so he could sit more comfortably with her naked, pulsating body, still impaled, and still under his total control.

He wrapped his arms around her. Her breath was warm against his neck. He could feel her breasts pressing against his chest. He smiled as men do when they're in love holding their woman, the woman he had just satisfied completely.

He had never been with a woman before. He had been talked into going to a brothel once, but changed his mind after seeing and smelling the woman. He knew without knowing how, that things should be different He could not force himself to cavort with an overly made-up, smelly whore. That wasn't the right way.

Gus later told him about love and how wonderful it made a man feel. Rubin wanted to have that feeling too. So he waited for this particular woman to share this magic moment. Life just changed for Rubin, it changed for Shadow too.

For a moment Rubin felt as though he had misused Shadow. Honor and integrity were paramount in the Wooesa tribe. The last thing he wanted to do was cause her shame or dishonor. But he smiled to himself, recollecting stories of other lovers needing and wanting each other so bad they could not wait for marriage. Looking at her in his arms, he could not imagine how love as strong as this could be wrong. He was in love with her and everything was right. The admission of love to himself for her made him harden even more inside her. She felt it and smiled.

He felt so much love for her he nearly cried. He gazed upon this small woman with wonder. He loved to hold and look at her small feet. Her hair was beautiful, silky and sexy. Her small nose turned up just enough to give her the face he adored. She had small hands, too. He couldn't stop looking at her, adoring everything about her. He touched and examined everything.

He looked up to the star-filled sky just as another streak of light traced across it. "Thank you, *Wankan Tanka*," he said reverently. A chorus of coyotes yipped and howled in reply. He kissed her forehead. "I love you, Shadow," he said softly to her. She had fallen into a trance and did not respond with words. Her eyes spoke to his soul telling him she was his.

He took her face in his hands again and kissed her savagely. He licked her lips and pushed his pelvis, just a bit, to penetrate her more deeply. He wanted to show her he was in charge and dominating her. Her eyes told him she could take him as rough as he wanted. She smiled, knowing she had found the lover she wanted.

CHAPTER THIRTY TWO

She thrust her hand out in a silent command to be still and silent. The movement startled Rubin but he froze in his tracks. He wouldn't even think of second-guessing her motives or desire. She said silently to hush and he would hush. He even willingly stood perfectly still, waiting for her signal to move, no matter how long it took. She wasn't moving at all now. She was however, watching something with the intensity of a cat, just inches away from pouncing on a mouse. No movement, no sound.

They had been out for a leisurely walk away from everyone and everything that could get in the way of their quiet, private time. They had been spending more time alone lately and enjoyed themselves as only young couples in love could. Always touching, caressing and holding. They explored faraway places they were certain no one else had ever been to. Heavily wooded areas or rocky ravines were their places of choice. They searched for those out-of-the-way places to guarantee their privacy. And when they found that certain place, they would join as one, if only for an hour or so.

But now something interfered. She had spotted something out there serious enough to warrant a command for silence and stillness. She must have felt danger present or she would not have behaved in such a manner. He had a knife, and his flintlock rifle. He could handle the knife well enough, but he knew his gun was good for little more than a club. It had yet to fire but still, he considered himself ready for anything.

She carried a staff she could use with lethal effectiveness. She also carried several knives stashed in inconspicuous places. She was always ready for anything. But, despite their combined strength and preparedness, he was scared. He was scared because she was scared. He had never seen her focused and poised for action in this manner before.

She motioned very slightly with only one finger for him to come closer. He did. He leaned over her shoulder, trying to see what she saw. He carefully lined his head up with hers. He thought he was facing the same way, looking along the same line she was, but he couldn't see anything. Then there was just the slightest movement.

Maybe it was a twitch of an animal's tail in the brush. Maybe it was the flutter of a bird's wing. He couldn't tell. He was once again amazed at Shadow's perception. Nothing got by her.

Then it moved again. This time he saw and identified it as the head of a man. The face could barely be seen through the camouflage he wore. Rubin became alarmed, wondering why anyone would try to hide, act so stealthily, in this expanse of uninhabited land. Rubin's breath became labored as adrenalin rushed through his body. He tried hard to better control his reactions, but failed. He was almost ashamed. Shadow had no outward signs of excitement. She was the perfect image of total composure despite being filled with fear and apprehension.

The hidden face turned slowly to look in their direction. Had they been spotted? Had he given their position away with his heavy breathing? He thought he saw two eyes blink behind the twigs and branches laced and woven around the face of the mysterious intruder. They had been noticed! But the unknown person was as controlled as Shadow was. Whoever it was, he slowly raised one hand, palm facing out, in a gesture of peace.

Rubin cursed himself after involuntarily clearing his throat. "Oh, well," he said softly, with a shrug.

"I've blown my cover." He couldn't help but smile at his tenderfoot behavior. Then he noticed with amazement that Shadow had slipped away from him totally unnoticed. "How does she do that," he muttered to himself. Wherever she was, he wasn't going to give her away.

He stepped slowly and deliberately from his place of concealment into the open, holding his hand up, palm facing out. "Ally, ally," he repeated. Then he said, in English, in his usual humorous tone. "Howdy!"

The other person, sitting on a bench-sized stone, now rose slowly to his feet, maintaining the hand gesture of peace. Slowly, he lifted the veil of camouflage from his face. They both looked at each other and blinked their eyes in astonishment.

"I don't believe it!" Rubin said.

They reached out to one another to embrace. Then they pushed away to look at each other, maintaining their hand clasp to slowly but very firmly shake hands.

"Captain Lewis, I can't believe I'm looking at you. How . . . why . . . out here?" Rubin was too flabbergasted to speak sensibly.

Captain Lewis put a calming hand on Rubin's shoulder. "I've much to explain." Meriwether Lewis looked at Rubin through troubled eyes. The former Captain smiled, but Rubin sensed his former expedition leader would have rather cried.

Captain Lewis, now Governor Lewis of the Louisiana Territory, put on a good act, yet Rubin saw through it. He knew this man well and he knew something troubled him. He didn't want to ask but had had to.

"What brings you out here and why all this?" He pointed to the camouflage face mask and the other branches of bushes and trees lashed to his clothing.

Governor Lewis began, in his well-educated and mannered tone, "Mr. Rubin, I am on a mission to try to right a few wrongs I am responsible for."

He perched his foot on the stone he had used for a seat, then rested his elbows on his elevated knee. He focused on a point unseen to anyone but him, a place in his mind enabling him to express himself more completely.

"While we were on the expedition, I became aware of a feeling quite unlike anything I had ever felt before. Even though we were on a mission to promote good will and cooperation between all the inhabitants of this land, I couldn't help but feel we were invading the Garden of Eden." He turned his head for a moment and looked at Rubin, his expression turning sorrowful. Then he added," I feel there will never be peace in this land, on this continent, because the white man is too caught up in the ideas of conquering and controlling. The white man will legislate to make laws and rules to serve him and will, with malice, legislate to keep them." He stopped to look at all that was around him. "The white man with his self-serving laws will keep the children of this land from what is rightfully theirs." Rubin nodded his head in understanding.

They sat and talked of times past and of times yet to come. Rubin had known Captain Lewis as an unusual person, educated far beyond Rubin's level, with a unique view of humanity and governments. There had been many occasions when Rubin listened intently to the man's visionary words. Meriwether Lewis had been not only the personal secretary of President Thomas Jefferson, but, for many years, had also been his close friend and confidante. Now he governed the Louisiana Territory, the largest single piece of land in the United States at the time.

Rubin trusted Mr. Lewis, but he was reluctant to call Shadow in. She knew better than he did about many things. He was new to intimate communication and relations with women and often wondered if all women were as intuitively accurate.

"I don't know why you feel threatened," Rubin said.

Governor Lewis told him his stealthy behavior was meant to minimize his exposure to others who may be trying to find him. "I felt I had to be honest with T.J., you know, Thomas Jefferson. I sent him a message I felt will be even more harmful than anything we've done thus far." Rubin cringed when he heard him say "we." He knew what they had done, that's why he was here.

"I came back here to try to redirect the coming prospectors and other vermin of the white culture." Saying this, he looked around suspiciously.

Rubin looked at him with questioning eyes. "Why don't you just come out and say what you are referring to? Don't keep me guessing." Rubin was growing impatient. Shadow still hadn't showed herself. Lewis explained that while on the expedition he had found mineral deposits giving him reason to believe gold might be somewhere nearby. After a little prospecting on his own, he had indeed found a rather large vein of what appeared to be gold. He left markers so he could easily relocate the site then sent a map and detailed notes back to President Jefferson. Later, after having second thoughts, he questioned the wisdom of his actions.

"I have a suspicion I will be confronted sometime soon. I've thought about how people will view my death. I've had more than one conversation on the subject of self-administered death you know. Should someone be able to kill me, it could be construed as self-administered." Rubin could only look at him with disbelief.

He and Rubin shared a long look at each other. Rubin remembered one of those conversations and wondered who else may have had the privilege of trust from such a respected man.

Meriwether concluded by saying, "People, white people, are anxious to find gold." A look of resignation showed on his face.

"These horrible, greedy people will do anything for easy wealth and the Indians are in their way." He fell silent for a long time. "I have done more to put these children of the earth into danger than any other man in history." He looked at Rubin with an expression of guilt.

They both sat in silent contemplation. Rubin thought carefully about his formal Captains actions. Maybe he should have felt more concerned but, deep inside he felt disconnected. He remembered the prophecy of Burning Tree about intentions and devices. And now Rubin was feeling the way he felt when he went over the waterfall with his brother. There really wasn't anything he could do. He just relaxed and waited for whatever may come next. He knew everything had its time and reason.

Mr. Lewis looked at Rubin with surprise. "You can see! . . . And you have spiritual knowledge, too!"

Rubin could only look at him, he had no words, his eyes spoke for him.

Lewis smiled, nodded his head approvingly, and said," I only want to know one thing from you, Mr. Rubin. When are you going to call your friend in and introduce me?"

Governor Lewis was amazed at Shadow's level of knowledge and education. He discovered she spoke French, English, and several dialects of Sioux. Her accent made her more unique and exotic in Rubin's opinion. Maybe Lewis thought so too. Governor Lewis was impressed with her overall view of politics, both in and out of Indian affairs and cultures.

He smiled as he looked at and assessed the love bond between Rubin and her. Mr. Lewis watched her watching Rubin with adoring eyes. He envied these two for the love they had found and wished someday, he might also have the most valued of treasures, love.

Meriwether Lewis was not a ladies' man. He had only one love in his life and she had politely refused his proposal of marriage. His smiles were always big and bright, but a sensitive eye could see the permanent pain dwelling within his soul.

He had been listening to Rubin talk about his transition from civilized white man to a Real Person. He looked at Rubin as he spoke but suddenly felt Shadow's penetrating eyes upon him. He looked at her and was stunned to see she was, in fact, looking at him and, at the same time, looking through him. She knew. He hung his head as if hiding. Shadow moved herself closer to him to sit at his side. She gently put her hand over his. She knew of and felt his pain of unanswered love. He looked away, afraid tears may soon streak his face. Rubin watched him struggle with his emotions. He wanted to help, but couldn't.

CHAPTER THIRTY THREE

With the first trace of morning light, the sun's orange orb began its slow rise from the edge of the earth. It did not rise up out of the ground as some believed thousands of years ago. The evolution of thought process was proceeding slowly, just as mountains were eroding into plains. As dawn lit the village, an assortment of songbirds provided gentle morning music to arouse dreamy sleepers. To see this inspiring sight only cost a person the effort of rising with the birds.

Animals seemed to be indifferent to the view, some seeing it as the signal for awakening and others for hiding out to sleep. People who meditated and communed with *The Creator* became habitual addicts of this mesmerizing sight.

It seemed supernatural yet, at the same time, perfectly normal. This mystical sight has always been, and will forever be inspiring. It was an orange ball brilliant in and of itself, casting not an orange light, but a soothing, ambient, calming light to welcome the freshly aroused sleepers to a new day.

These marvelous moments of the morning hours will always inspire, heal, motivate, and grow in fertile minds, understanding of the unspoken yet clearly heard words of *God*, the *Creator, Wankan Tanka*. That is, unless you are sound asleep, snoring loudly, as Rubin was doing this particular morning.

As the sun climbed upward, it warmed the land quickly. Rubin kicked off the animal hides with which he covered himself as his tipi began to heat up. The soft stirring of humans, mixed with the distant sounds of horses rummaging about with hobbled legs, declared that morning had broken. Horses knew daylight meant being turned out to open fields to graze. They rapidly grew anxious and whinnied with impatience.

All of these soft morning sounds mixed into a gentle medley rising up from the valley. The morning chorus created a relaxing, good-natured atmosphere. It was a beautiful and peaceful way to wake up, a natural alarm clock.

He casually rolled around on a comfortable pallet of animal hides. These sights and sounds stirred a question of his inner self, "Why live anywhere else or any other way?" His contentment was complete. All he wanted now was Shadow sharing his tipi and his life with him.

Suddenly, the soft sounds changed to loud and frantic noises, growing louder and more frantic by the second. "This is too early for so much commotion," he muttered with irritation. Pulling an antelope hide over his head he tried unsuccessfully to ignore the rowdy early birds.

"I give up," He shouted, knowing it was useless to try and relax any longer. The entire village seemed to be rallying to some singular event. Something serious was going on.

The commotion reminded him of the day of his introduction to the village. He sat up abruptly. "Maybe they've found Joe!" He prepared hurriedly with hopeful anticipation. Excitement filled him by the second as he jumped to his feet, stumbling from the tipi, trying to put his boots on. He continued his stumbling act as he joined in the pandemonium.

Much to his dismay, the commotion wasn't about Joe. He slowly expelled a deflated sigh. His shoulders sagged involuntarily. "Too much to hope for, I guess," he said in a low tone.

The real center of excitement was an Indian who had either wandered in or been found and brought in. Rubin only caught a brief glimpse of the newcomer through the gathering crowd. But that momentary glimpse revealed a man who had either been severely beaten or had been attacked by a bear or something equally menacing. The injured Indian was saying things Rubin couldn't understand. He was certain the Indian spoke Sioux, but still . . . maybe it was a different dialect. Whatever he was saying, it caused Thunder Horse to respond with firm orders to his people.

A small party of warriors immediately mounted their horses and rode off. The injured Indian thrashed and shouted, hindering the efforts of the villagers trying to help him. He was trying very hard to make something understood. Finally, he was carried away, still ranting, to a lodge where he would be cared for.

Chief Thunder Horse waved his arms as he gave instructions. People hurried about on the specific tasks he assigned them. Burning Tree, at the Chief's side, watched quietly, followed closely, but remained silent.

As the crowd began to break up, Rubin realized he was on the receiving end of hostile looks from people he knew and considered being on great terms with.

But now a few people were acting like had done something wrong. He became even more concerned when he heard harsh tones directed toward him. He was for the second time since he had arrived, scared of the tribe.

The crowd dispersed rapidly, leaving Rubin standing alone and full of questions. Had there been a confrontation with Captain Lewis? Had something happened with the people Mr. Lewis worried about? Disturbing scenarios flooded his mind.

Rubin began to feel uneasy two days ago as he and Shadow bade Mr. Lewis farewell. He knew trouble was on the way. But he didn't know what form it would take.

It was late in the day before Rubin was able to see Shadow. She had been busy helping her mother with chores in their family tipi. Lately she had been neglecting her home and family. Being his translator required much of her time. Her mother was getting behind with the maintenance of the family tipi and the care typically given to the elders living with them. She had explained her situation to Rubin, asking him to understand.

He had never called to her from outside her family's tipi before. He knew she was occupied with other commitments, but he needed her now.

When she was in her home with her parents, he thought it would be most polite to wait until she came out before approaching her. But his concern about the morning events caused him to grow impatient.

He called out, "Shadow, are ya in there?" He stood outside by the entrance, hat in hand. With a look of surprise on her face, she came out through the flap that served as a door, her mother right behind her. Shadow greeted Rubin. Her mother looked over her shoulder, her face reflecting her suspicion. He greeted her mother with sincere respect.

Shadow's mother invited him in to sit by the hearth with her parents. Hospitality was the rule of their clan. Despite some unspoken bad feelings, all members greeted him as he entered the tipi.

The tipi was surprisingly large and very tall. Shadow lived there with her parents, an uncle, two aunts, and a grandfather from each side of the family. She had two older brothers, but they lived elsewhere. The tipi was warm, and well organized. All visitors were treated with courtesy and respect. He greeted every member of her family before he sat in the place reserved for a guest.

Then he spoke to Shadow. "You're the only one who can tell me what happened this morning." He looked at her pleadingly. "Something bad happened and I feel like I'm being blamed."

"I don't know much. But the scout who came in said a village had been massacred."

"A whole village massacred!" He repeated in disbelief. "Are ya sure?"
Shadow nodded her head sadly.

He asked her, "By white people?" He looked into the eyes of her parents. They were looking at him suspiciously. Again Shadow nodded.

Rubin sighed and hung his head. "Now I know why everyone is acting the way they are."

"More will be known when the other scouts return," she told him. She reached out and put her hand on his arm and gave him a small, sympathetic squeeze.

Rubin struggled for sound reasoning behind this report. Had there been provocation? This was Indian territory. That should rule out a military attack. He sat silently, like her parents, considering the situation. The natives of this land were generally kind and curious, making them easy targets to try and take advantage of. The French had been in this part of the country for generations and were trusted. Other whites, like himself were struggling for acceptance.

It was the frontier people from the east who were more untrustworthy. The Indians were just beginning to figure this out, thus the suspicious looks from everyone. He was the image of what they feared, a white man they learn to trust, then get betrayed by him.

The scouting party returned two days later. They went directly to the community circle. Chief Thunder Horse and all the council members of the village rapidly gathered. The sweat covered snorting horses of the scouts were led away. It took only minutes before the whole village had assembled around that circle, waiting for word of what they had learned. Dust rose from the feet of the shuffling villagers and running dogs.

The scouts divulged their findings. The look of astonishment and bewilderment on the faces of the villagers was apparent. The scouts told of a horrible scene of mutilated bodies and destroyed homes. Shadow struggled to listen. Rubin fidgeted nervously, not daring to break her concentration by speaking.

Everyone listened. Shadow spoke to several people before she revealed to Rubin what she had heard. He took his turn asking questions. His patience was being tested. There was just so much he had to learn, and it seemed like time was running out.

"The scouts have been to a village a night and day ride from here. It is —" She paused for thought and reflection. "—It was a village of peaceful people farther toward the rising sun. She looked deep into his eyes. "The village was burned and all the people slain. It appeared it was done suddenly and without cause." She added that they found the villagers had not waged a defensive fight. There were no dead white people.

"They must have been taken by surprise. Possibly someone they knew and trusted came in. The scouts believe the people responsible for this have made camp just a day's ride from here. They fear they will come here next." She looked at him with worried eyes.

"How do the scouts know it was white people who did this?" He asked.

"The wounds on the villagers were done with weapons that our people do not have," she answered.

Her eyes were wide with alarm. She had never known an invasion of her clan. The entire village began to reverberate with the sound of panic.

Defensive preparations were being carried out in the village. Instructions for splitting up and hiding in different places were given. Warrior braves formed a defensive perimeter ring around the village. Survival supplies were taken away and hidden. Families made their own plans for splitting up and regrouping at a different place later. Thunder Horse was overwhelmed. He and his clan, calling themselves the Wooesa, have known peace for generations. He didn't know how to handle this situation properly.

Rubin suddenly became aware of something very important. He held Shadows hand and together they ran to the Chief.

"Tell him to remember all the conversations we had about the bad qualities we agreed I have. Ask him to remember all those bad things we couldn't figure out what good they were for, tell him I just found out what they are good for. Tell him I know how to defend against these invaders. *Tell him I know why I'm here.*"

Rubin stopped as Shadow continued here translation. A feeling surged through his body. He's been here before. He saw it looking into the setting sun in the mouth of the cave on the Lewis and Clark expedition. He saw it looking into the eyes of the dying Indian. He saw it sailing through the cosmos with Mountain Wind. It was clear now, those were test for him. All his experiences, all his lessons with Burning Tree were designed to put him here now. He was here for a specific reason. He was going to save the *Wooesa*.

Thunder Horse listened to Shadow translate the words from the *Man With Important Messages*, *The Man Who Stands in Water*. He looked at Rubin with a new found respect. Thunder Horse heard many times, the story of the one who would come and save them and set them on a new direction. He was moved and touched by the spirit of Rubin. Thunder Horse wondered if maybe he wasn't being a witness for the first time in his life of a white man turning into *A Real Person*. He began to chant and dance.

Rubin had been through military training and recognized an opportunity to apply knowledge he harbored to help this tribe. He knew now, for the first time what his destiny was. He was here to help this tribe, a tribe of kindred souls he now considered himself part of.

He understood the strategic philosophy of the defense of the core. *The Wooesa* was the core and it had to be saved at all cost. But once again, communication was the ever present barrier. It was vital he make the villagers trust and believe in him. And now he needed Shadow more than ever.

She translated to a large crowd Thunder Horse had call together. She stressed how important it was for them to listen to Rubin so they would be able to protect themselves and survive. "Rubin knows why we, *The Wooesa*, are a target."

He watched and listened to her and realized she had become a part of himself, and he had become a part of her. They were a team. Rubin smiled and said softly to himself, "ain't love crazy."

He listened to her tell them, "We have the power to visit and learn from our *Creator*. Some men from the east believe that they, and only they, can commune with and understand *The Creator*. They believe it is their duty to tell people how to live according to the laws and rules only they can hear and see. It's hard for us to understand how or why living in peace and harmony can be twisted and used for control. We must survive so that we may point the way to seeing and hearing the words and actions of our *Great Creator, Wankan Tanka.*"

Rubin asked her to also tell them, "The white people from the east do not see what you see. I come from a place where people believe terrible things about you. They are wrong but they will act wrongfully believing they are right. They will trick you to trust them then they will take advantage of you."

The crowd chattered as they studied Rubin. Thunder Horse eyed Rubin with pride. A battle plan was made. Explanations and directions were rapidly given. Groups were made and dispatched to different settings. The situation was difficult until a young brave, who also knew some English stopped and asked Rubin, "We have learned to live in peace, why are we now learning to fight."

It was a reality check. Rubin needed to hear an answer from himself as much as this young man needed to hear it. Rubin started with his relaxed body language and slow speech. "The way I see and understand it, we all have our own idea of what a good life should be like. I've learned that some people have plans that could mean pain and suffering for others. I don't want to be a part of that kind of person's life or plan.

I don't know how to make things better for anybody and I'm not sure I should change things if I could. I believed I was doing something great once. I was on an expedition and thought all the time I was on it that I was doing something great for our nation, great for humanity. Fact is, I might be responsible for future problems because of what I did. It's hard for me to think too far in advance, so I just watch and listen to the signs that guide me.

I've seen *God*, *Wankan Tanka*, and life was revealed to me. I only know that whatever is going on is a process that takes longer than the life of a mountain. I've had guidance to be here and I know that defending yourself to survive, and fighting for peace and what you believe in is sometimes necessary. It's *the code of life*."

The young Indian brave listened and understood. He stepped back, raised his bow and said, "We will defend our peace." He ran to his assigned post with a new conviction.

Rubin went over the battle strategy in his mind very carefully. He defined the defensive perimeter, point and timing of attack, and path of retreat. "*Lead by example.*" That's what Captain Clark said. Rubin could hear his old friend and leader saying, "If you want people to follow you, you have to lead the way. Show them you know what you're doing and radiate confidence."

He and Shadow instructed the fighting men about the strategies of battle. It was difficult at first because the Indians thought of battle differently than white men do. They strove to maintain pride and dignity in battle. "The white man will trick you into believing they are harmless and come in peace. They will press every advantage," Rubin told them.

The Indians listened to Rubin with respectful attention. They were good people who believed in him. They looked at him with imploring eyes. He looked back into the eyes of least two hundred men. "I came here on a mission to tell all the Real People of the white man's deceptive ways. I came here to warn of much trouble and death. I can lead you to victory over those who wish you harm." Shadow's energetic tone sent Rubin's words into the crowd. A stunning, warrior's cheer rose in a unified voice.

Training was simple. They had basic weapons and they used them very well. Yet they needed to work as one. Teaching them, in a crash course to follow directions was paramount. To be victorious, they were told to watch for certain formations and to attack at intervals, and then rapidly retreat. Being honorable people, this was difficult for them to grasp. They were also taught to have a decoy group, with an ambush group waiting. Having only an estimate of the number of intruders concerned Rubin. This was not a battle to count coup; this was a matter of life and death.

The Indians were brave enough, but that was both a blessing and a problem. It didn't matter if they were outnumbered twenty-to-one. They believed the worse the odds, the better. They learned very early that being brave was the most important virtue a man could have.

He was trying to teach them, in a crash course, to use intelligence with their bravery.

A scout ran into the village shouting about a line of horses he had seen coming from the rising sun. He expected them to arrive before noon. The horsemen were wearing white frocks marked with red crosses, holding their banners high on long poles. Their weapons included flintlock rifles, swords and lances.

Thunder Horse and Burning Tree stood close by one another in constant council with each other. Children and women scurried away to their hiding places. Warrior braves prepared their mounts and themselves for a hostile encounter.

"It's time to take command," Rubin said to himself

CHAPTER THIRTY FOUR

One hundred and forty determined-looking, self-righteous men rode up to the village. Their faces appeared as masks depicting prejudicial hatred. Ready for murder, they carried sabers, lances, and flintlock firearms. The leader of this ragtag army was Father Andrew Bartholomew Ross. The Catholic priest had convinced this band of derelicts to follow and obey his unholy, demented commands to seek out and destroy all Indians unwilling or unable to convert from their way of life and worship to that of his. The men wore sheets painted with a red cross. Father Ross wore a white satin frock embellished by an embroidered cross, also in red. Spattered, dried drops of blood stained his white garment.

The men quickly spread themselves out around the edges of the village. Several banner carriers proudly held poles displaying their coveted slogans and motifs. The flags gently flapped in the mild breeze as the group came to a unified halt.

Chief Thunder Horse observed this formation from his place on the ground, watching as they tried to cut off all escape routes. The mounted crusaders believed they held the village in an impossible position.

Fortunately for the *Wooesa*, these hostile riders had chosen a late morning encounter. If they had ridden in at daybreak, Rubin's warriors would not have been ready. Fate was once again conspiring to help him with his missions.

The added time allowed him to place his warriors at strategic locations and give last minute advice. The village men, women, and children were as ready as they could possibly be.

All that could be heard was the snorting of horses and the barking of dogs, restrained somewhere out of sight.

The brutal looking riders exchanged looks of satisfaction as they surveyed the village. They sensed an easy kill and a rewarding pillage. Thunder Horse would not let his apprehension show. He stood rigidly before them, proud and defiant.

The invading riders studied the situation. These were savage men, but they weren't stupid. It slowly dawned on them that something was not right. There were fewer Indians than expected. There were too many lodges and tipis, not enough people. And they could hear restrained dogs, but couldn't see them. That didn't fit. Dogs were always underfoot in an Indian village. This wasn't like the last village they raided. That village was crowded. The people had been curious and trusting. They had invited Reverend Ross and his men into their village believing they were going to openly discuss *The Great Creator*. They were wrong.

After Ross's men had infiltrated that village they systematically neutralized any threat or opportunity to defend or resist. The interrogations began. "Who are the *Wooesa* and where can they be found?" Ross demanded from the subdued villagers.

The peaceful villagers found themselves caught in a living hell. Nightmarish torture began. Ross scolded himself for not bring an interpreter with him. When communication failed, dying began. In the chaos, one Indian crawled away. Destiny provided a path for a survivor to warn *The Wooesa*.

Something was not right here, but they didn't know what it was. Some Indians carried on with their usual activities. A few horses were tethered nearby, but not enough for a village this size. That confused the raiders most. The villagers were going about their usual business and acted unconcerned. Several people could be seen farther out in the community garden working, also seemingly uninterested in the developing situation. It wasn't quite normal, it wasn't what they expected, but they hadn't visited — or destroyed — enough villages to be sure. There were just enough normalcies to pacify the intruders, but just barely. Yet they knew something about the situation was wrong.

A nervous rider next to Father Ross leaned over to converse with him. Father Ross, a savage-looking man in his own way, with greasy, matted hair and an oily perspiring face, nodded his head as if approving a request.

Chief Thunder Horse stood midway between the band of riders, his village and people. The rider left the side of Father Ross and rode to meet him, jumping down to the ground in front of the Chief. Thunder Horse greeted the lone rider by holding his hand up in the sign of peace. He wore his headdress, the long feathered cape hanging down his back. It divided into two tails that touched the ground. He was an impressive man.

Rubin observed the priest's spokesman from concealment hearing the harshly spoken words. The rider demanded to inspect the village. Thunder Horse looked confused but, before he could question or object, the rider jumped back onto his horse and rode off, galloping his horse through the entire village. He was suspicious. It was too quiet and there weren't enough people around. He returned to Thunder Horse.

The lone rider spoke. "Where are all your people, your horses?" Chief Thunder Horse stood still, not answering. He looked at the intruders, intensely scrutinizing them. "I know you have more people than what I see. Where are they?" he asked in a demanding voice.

The demented priest rode up and interrupted with words of his own. "We have come to spread the word of salvation through the acceptance of the Word of Jesus Christ." He paused for a moment. "Are you ready to accept the Word of *God*, and take Jesus Christ as your Savior?"

Chief Thunder Horse could not understand the words being said to him. In his language he replied, "You are welcome here, if you come in peace."

The priest scowled, not understanding the language. Angered by the Chief's inability to speak English, he raised his voice. "Will you surrender your savage ways and accept the will of *God* and live your lives in a Christian way, or will you choose to perish?"

Chief Thunder Horse shook his head and shrugged his shoulders. Then he implored, "We are peaceful people and wish to live in peace with all the children of *Maka*." He held his hands out in a pleading manner. The priest and his companion rider misunderstood the gestures of the Chief as aggressive.

The villagers, hiding away in the crevices of rocky ledges, inside tipis, and within thinly wooded areas, stirred nervously. Those who had stayed in the nearly deserted village had done so as a show of force, as instructed by Rubin, to try and deceive the marauders into believing they had cornered and were confronting all the occupants of the village. Others, hiding in tipis and lodges, were armed and ready to repel aggression, if needed. They awaited a verbal command from Rubin. The lone rider's horse stamped and snorted, shaking its head furiously as if in defiance of Thunder Horse. Dangerous, threatening looks were exchanged between Thunder Horse and the rider.

The rider lost his patience and shouted out his condemnation to the Chief. "You have denied the will of *God* and you will pay for your sins with your life." He and the priest rode hastily back to the line of his comrades.

Chief Thunder Horse looked back at his village and gave a silent," prepare," command with a hand signal. The villagers who had stayed, and those in the garden area, moved to their defensive positions, although it was not yet obvious that they were doing so.

Father Ross slowly rode his horse back to Chief Thunder Horse. He wore a smug smirk on his face that revealed his true, inner self.

"I'll give you the same warning I gave to the last few villages we visited, fall on your knees and humbly accept the word of Christ and we'll allow you and your people to live. Hesitate or resist and you and all your people will perish." He smiled broadly.

The Chief shook his head in confusion but tried to explain his point. He held out his hands with open palms.

"Do you not see we are peaceful people who wish to live in harmony with all the living creatures *Wankan Tanka* has put here? We wish harm to no one. We will gladly share what we have with you." He was desperately trying to communicate with his tone, knowing his language would not be understood.

This deliberate attempt by the Chief to connect, person to person, soul to soul, was a dangerous gamble, but one the Chief thought he had to take. Written words were too easily violated by deliberate misrepresentation or misunderstanding. The only contract the Chief of the Wooesa would honor would be a contract made by the soul of a sincere person. It was the only contract he knew was binding. He didn't know he was trying to reason with a madman.

Shadow could take no more. She had been standing inside a nearby tipi, listening carefully. The Chief had ordered her to stay back unless she was called to translate. He worried for her safety. Words meant little if a man's soul was not sincere. And if the man was sincere, then words were not necessary. The Chief had a bad feeling about these people. He didn't want Shadow in harm's way.

She didn't know why he didn't call for her but she felt she had to do something before things got any father out of hand. She ran up to her Sachem. "Forgive me," she said in Sioux to her Chief, her Sachem. She gave him a quick half-bow. Then she spoke in English to the priest. "I speak white face." She translated quickly to Andrew Ross what her Chief had said. Thunder Horse looked at her with adoring eyes. He knew what she was trying to do and could see, once again, how fearless and determined she was. Even under these circumstances, he could not refrain from smiling at her. He slowly shook his head in disbelief at the tenacity of this young woman. He beamed with pride. He knew she, and others like her, were the future of his people, however short that future might be.

Father Ross saw the Chief shaking his head and took it as an act of defiance. "Just what I thought," he snarled. "Just like the others." His hand had been under his frock. He pulled it out to reveal a gun. "No!" Shadow screamed. The priest fired.

The band of degenerate thugs took the gun shot as their signal to begin their assault, charging into the village while screaming and firing their guns. Villagers spewed from tipis and lodges, surprising the assailants. Arrows held at the ready now took flight. Screams of misery and torment began to fill the air.

Shadow knelt by her fallen Chief. She cradled his head in her hands. "My Sachem," she cried.

He looked at her and smiled. "You will be the one to carry the seed of our people away." His smiled broadened as he struggled to speak. "Let not this evil side of the white man shape your world. All is as it should be." He choked and fixed his gaze upon her.

Then he looked past her to see a mounted Indian riding up fast with another spirited horse on a tether. They rode up to Shadow and the mortally wounded chief. The father of Thunder Horse looked down at him. He had a tight smile on his face and nodded for his son, Chief Thunder Horse, to join him. He handed the braided reins down to the dying Chief.

The Chief reached up to touch to reins and, when he did, he was instantly mounted on a snorting horse. The horse then reared up on its hind legs and whinnied. Thunder Horse looked at his father with amazement. They had hunted and explored together for many years when he was alive. Now they both looked down at the sight of Shadow holding the spent body of her Sachem. Shadow couldn't see the two young, handsome spirits.

"Yee, Yaa!" the Chief screamed.

"Yee, Yaa!" his father replied with equal enthusiasm.

They kicked their horses and rode into the sky. He and his father looked down through the clouds and saw an eagle flying below them. The eagle looked up at them and screamed with a high pitch. They laughed as they did when they had shared time together, when they both lived. They kicked at their horses and rode into the other world.

Shadow bowed her head and cried over her beloved chief. She willed herself to recover quickly. It was none too soon. Out of the corner of her eye she saw a rider charging at her with a drawn saber held high. He slashed at her while riding by. He missed her, but not by much. Maddened by rage she pulled the knife from the belt of Thunder Horse and jumped to her feet. In one fluid motion she threw the knife backhanded. The rider threw his hands up and fell from his horse with the knife buried deep in his back.

Rubin was running about holding his hands up, shouting out orders, trying to stop the carnage. Several white riders rode past him without considering him a target. They probably thought him an Indian captive, grateful for deliverance.

The marauding riders did exactly what Rubin had expected. They separated to begin targeted attacks. Three rode out toward the horse keepers, a strategy to limit mobility. They only lived for a short time. A dozen Indians, waiting anxiously, obscured by squash leaves, stood up suddenly and let their arrows fly. All the riders fell to the ground with several arrows embedded in each of them.

Then Rubin motioned the first group of villagers to run toward nearby stone formations. Premeasured distances allowed for perfectly timed retreats. As expected, they were chased. Just as the running Indians reached the stone formations, they fell to the ground. The assailants rode in fast and close, their sabers raised ready to slaughter. They never saw the Indians jumping from behind the stones. The riders were easy targets for these archers sending deadly, penetrating arrows into them at very close range.

One of the tipis had been set on fire. A young mother ran out of it holding her baby lashed to a cradle board. A flintlock rifle erupted and the young mother fell to the ground dead, her baby screaming. No sooner had that shooter fired than an Indian ran, jumped, and mounted that rider's horse from behind him. The Indian brave quickly slashed the shooter's throat and pushed his body to the ground. He lay there jerking as blood sprayed from his cut arteries.

Shadow ran toward the fallen mother, picking up a bow and a quiver of arrows from a fallen villager as she ran. She grabbed the baby with one well-practiced motion and swung the cradle board over her shoulder.

Straddling the dead mother, she laced her arms through the shoulder straps as she fitted an arrow, drew and released. A rider clutched at the shaft buried in his chest, tumbling off his horse.

Quickly Rubin pulled the ramrod from the barrel of his gun. He felt immune from attack. His skin color protected him. He kept his focus on Shadow. She was shooting arrows as fast as she could find targets within range. A horseman focused on her. He was galloping toward her with his saber held high. Shadow didn't see him. Rubin prayed as he raised his rifle. "Oh, dear God, please don't let this gun misfire this time. If ever it needs to fire, it needs to be now!"

A tremendous explosion of gunpowder and a kick as strong as a mule told him his prayers had been answered. He couldn't see through the smoke for a few seconds but when the smoke finally cleared, he saw Shadow standing there looking at the body that had fallen just a few feet away from her. "Well I'll be darned," he said in a low voice.

Shadow turned her head to look at Rubin. A look of rage on her face made him think she misunderstood his intention. "I wasn't shooting at you," he yelled. "Hell woman, I love you, I wouldn't hurt you."

She rapidly drew her bowstring back and let an arrow fly straight toward him. He was so stunned at this action he couldn't move. He felt the breeze from the arrow as it sailed inches from his face. He turned with a shaking motion to see where the arrow went. A man behind him, ready to split him open with his saber, carried the arrow in his neck. The saber fell as the man grabbed at the shaft, and then he fell. Rubin trembled.

Slowly he turned back around to see a smiling, beautiful woman looking straight at him. She mouthed the words, "I love you too."

He read those lips and smiled. His life was complete. He thought about holding her, loving her, and living with her. He was standing in the middle of a battle field with death and madness all around him and he was smiling. "Ain't love crazy," he thought.

The attack quickly ended. The priest fled at a full gallop, his few surviving raiders following as fast as they could. The surviving villagers raised their hands and cheered. Rubin ran to Shadow and took her in his arms. Their kiss lasted till the cheers faded away.

Rubin looked around him and saw all the senseless death. Growling, he cursed with anger. He searched the horizon for the sight of the fleeing priest. He and the other villagers saw the priest and his men riding away. Then they watched in fascination as they were overtaken by a mysterious group of riders.

"What do you suppose that's all about?" Rubin asked. Shadow shook her head. The riders were soon out of sight.

Preparation and ceremony for burial was emotional. Many of the Indians howled and wept. Rubin struggled hard not to weep as they wrapped the body of their Chief, their friend. He was stunned when he was led away to a large, brightly burning fire. Burning Tree, who had survived the attack, talked to Rubin in a tone heard by all the people of the village. Shadow was by his side to translate. The Shaman said, "You have shown much courage and wisdom. You are truly one of the Real People." He took Chief Thunder Horse's headdress and placed it on Rubin's head. "Thunder Horse had no son. He claimed you as his child!" The entire village began to softly stamp their feet and chant as one.

CHAPTER THIRTY FIVE

After the assault on the village, interrogation of two of the surviving marauders disclosed information about Father Ross, his disposition, and his agenda. The villagers were angered. They felt pity for these short-sighted, easily misdirected men. A suggestion to send these men walking alone, unarmed, into the wilderness was considered. Only Rubin prevented it. He argued passionately that it would be better to send these men back where they came from with a message. He wanted them to tell people everywhere the Indians were eager to live in peace and wished no harm to anyone.

It was difficult for Shadow to support Rubin's argument that these men should live. He understood her feelings, but, as one of *The Real People*, he couldn't see a benefit to sending the men into the wilderness unarmed. That would most likely be a death sentence. Killing them, even in this fashion would place *The Wooesa* on their level, making a statement saying their connection to The Great Spirit was meaningless.

After Shadow and other villagers, thought, saw and heard the two captives' remorse, they agreed with Rubin. The men cried and pleaded, not for the salvation of their lives, but for the forgiveness of their sins. They seemed truly sorry. Shadow believed they could do more for the plight of her people by staying alive. She then realized how sensitive Rubin had become, and how right he was. Her love, respect, and admiration for him grew more than she ever thought possible.

The two men were released with a blessing, a command to be of service to all people of *Maka*, and a hope that their lives would be filled with mercy. They swore they would be. Of course, they left the village with only their knives in their possession. As Yumni had done before them, they would walk until they found civilization. All their other weapons and horses now belonged to the village.

With their release, Rubin grew anxious. He told Shadow, "I've just got to try and find out what happened to their leader. They were dressed like Christian Crusaders. He had to be the Father Ross I heard about before leaving St. Louis." Shadow studied him as she listened. "Besides, he and the rest of his men, if still together, could yet be out there, regrouping for another attack." Shadow's eyes flared with alarm. "We have to find out," he said in conclusion. She reluctantly nodded her head in agreement.

The next morning they set out with provisions, complete with some of the firearms acquired from the marauders. Three very capable warriors escorted Rubin and Shadow. He considered them insurance as well as messengers. They would take information back to the village should the situation turn threatening. And Rubin found their strength and abilities reassuring. Burning Tree blessed them before they left.

They picked up the trail at the point they last saw the riders. They counted at least a dozen unshod horses, plus other shod ones. The unshod were Indian horses; the others had to be Father Ross's army of thugs. The three warriors accompanying them smiled among themselves, speaking in low whispers.

"Well, what's the joke, what's so funny," Rubin asked with a hint of aggravation.

They shrugged their shoulders but it didn't remove the grins from their faces.

Shadow hadn't heard the warriors, but she heard Rubin. She, too, became agitated and demanded they tell her what they thought was so humorous.

"Angry Bear," they said.

CHAPTER THIRTY SIX

Rubin hadn't seen or heard of Angry Bear for a long time. It was a month or so before he realized the taunts and threatening gestures, once an everyday event, were missing from his daily routines. When he asked, he was told Angry Bear had gone but would return. Rubin enjoyed the peace while he could.

Shadow now told him Angry Bear had left the village permanently because she refused to marry him. About a dozen loyal braves, and some women, went with him to start another tribe. "Angry Bear leaves in anger. Makes sense to me," Rubin said with a smile. "I couldn't imagine an Angry Bear leaving as a happy bear." His sense of humor kept Shadow, and others, smiling. And it was good that his nemesis was gone. But were these the tracks of Angry Bear and his band?

The trail was easy to follow. It didn't take them long to discover the answers to their questions. Their doubts and nervous apprehension were alleviated. They could see what had happened, they didn't need to go any farther. But they did. Slowly, they moved closer to the far end of a boxed, sandstone canyon. The canyon was narrow, but deep, with steep sides.

There, with a beautiful backdrop of naturally painted sandstone, was Father Ross and his men. He had been lashed, upright, to a large boulder.

He was stretched and spread as far as his limbs would allow. His men were staked to the ground.

Dismounting, they took the final steps to stand beside the man they knew had led the band of marauders. Rubin was sure it was Father Ross when he saw the Bible laying near one of the dead man's feet. The white satin smock, with its red cross, was lashed to the other side of the boulder, stretched to its limits as well.

All Rubin could think to say as he stared in horror was, "Why?" Not a question as to why he was lashed to the boulder and tortured to death, but a question as to why he did what he did. Rubin had seen this man kill without remorse or conscience. He saw this man alive and full of hate. It was unbelievable.

This was a man of the *Cloth*. He could still see hate in the eyes that stared blankly up at the burning afternoon sun. They could not close. The eyelids were gone, most likely the first thing they cut off after he was lashed down. They had wanted him to see everything. His skin had been cut in a dozen different places, and then pulled down to his waist in small, thin strips. Those strips of flesh were dried now. They looked like long hairs coming out of his side. Something had been rubbed into the cuts to keep him from bleeding to death. They wanted him to last a long time. His testicles and ears had been removed, too. During all this, he could not have screamed or cursed. His tongue was missing.

"Let's cut him down and bury him," Rubin said. He was nearly sick at the sight and couldn't handle the thought of what this man must have gone through before his death. Yet, Rubin believed all people deserved burial at death. He reached out to cut the sinew that held the man's wrists and ankles.

"Hiya! Hiya!" came a loud command, meaning "No! No!" "You cannot have him. He is mine," proclaimed Angry Bear, finality in his voice. He had been hiding behind another boulder, listening, watching. He was covered in dried blood. The other members of his band slowly made themselves known, silently stepping from their hiding places. They, too, were covered with dried blood.

He pointed to Shadow. "You have taken heart of Angry Bear." Rubin knew Shadow had never wanted to be part of Angry Bear's life. He knew Angry Bear had tried in vain to win her love and affection. She had rejected him totally.

"Now you want man who kills my people," he jumped into Rubin's face and screamed. "You cannot have!" Shadow was shouting the translation to Rubin. Then she said something else to Angry Bear, something very personal, It made him growl. Then Shadow stepped close to Rubin and took his hand. She pressed her body close to his and raised her leg up across the front of his waist. Angry Bear screamed. Rubin had a good idea what she may have said to him. The body language said the rest. Rubin almost felt sorry for Angry Bear. Almost.

The vicious way in which the priest had been killed, and the way Angry Bear claimed the body, was enough to convince Rubin he wasn't going to cut down anyone for burial.

"Okay, Angry Bear," Rubin said in a submissive tone. He didn't want any more bloodshed. Though the braves with him would have fought at his command, he decided to back off and let Angry Bear have his victory. "It's all yours," he said, nodding to the lifeless body. He and Shadow, and their three escorts, slowly backed up, mounted their horses, and rode back to the village.

CHAPTER THIRTY SEVEN

Side by side, they sat upon their horses. They faced the slow flowing Elkhorn River. They scanned with squinted eyes up and down the river searching for . . . anything. "Home is around here somewhere," Rubin said cheerfully. "I think if we go down here a little bit more we'll find a house or cattle or something that'll show we're there. Home, I mean." Shadow looked into his eyes as though she was looking into his head. "I asked you not to look at me that way, darling." He knew she doubted his judgment.

"We go that way," she pointed in the opposite direction.

He shook his head. "No, Shadow, we go this way." He pointed back down the river.

"Wrong way," she replied. She was mounted. Her horse was close enough to his horse that she could take her reins and slap at his leg. "Is wrong way, is not even right river," she said, nearly shouting.

They could have sat there all day disagreeing, but Shadow relented with a smile that tells a man he is in deep mud, if he's wrong. He swallowed hard before he said, "I'm glad you agree with me, my love." He was sweating and it wasn't because he was hot.

"Shadow not agree. Shadow let man be foolish." She said "man" but, in her language, that meant "men," plural, all men.

The pressure was on and Rubin felt like he was trying to bluff with a pair of deuces. It was manly pride that made him go his way and he hated it. He felt deep down she was right, but just couldn't give in and say something intelligent, like, "You might be right. Let's try it your way." The farther they rode, the worse he felt.

They covered many miles and nothing even remotely resembling any kind of settlement showed up. Shadow watched him closely but said nothing. They camped for the night. She slept with her back toward him.

After an unusually quiet morning meal, Rubin burst out with an excited explanation. "I know where we wrong! Do you remember, about thirty miles back, the large cactus that looked like a horse laying on its back with its legs sticking straight up in the air?" Turning his head, he looked at her. "Remember that?" Shadow watched him in disbelief. Then he jumped up, slapped his knee and said, 'Well, we should have rode west instead of east at that place."

She had a hard time getting mad at him. And when she did get mad, she couldn't stay mad at him even though she tried. He was just too funny. He didn't let the little problems in life get him upset. She liked that very much. She tackled him, holding him tightly in her arms, lying on top of him. "I take my husband to home soon," she said, kissing him. He returned her kisses.

They had been married by Burning Tree, just before they left the village of *The Wooesa*. The hot spark from their kisses kindled a fire. That burning fire turned into hot lovemaking.

It was late in the day and they had covered about fifty miles, crossed seven creeks, including one that was very deep and swift, and rode past one bluff with a tremendous pile of buffalo bones at the bottom. Shadow told Rubin this was the bottom of one of the run-offs hunters used, where they would slowly and patiently drive, then stampede, a herd of buffalo over the edge. He looked up. It was a fall of about eighty feet. It was high enough to be crippling or lethal.

When a hunt like this took place, many groups had to work together harvesting meat and hides. Fires and drying racks spread over several acres. Hides covered every available inch left on the ground, being dried and cured. The bones were used for tools and weapons for hunting. All the butchering was done right there. What couldn't be used was left behind for the animals to scavenge, thus the pile of unusable bones.

They came to another dry gully. Shadow pointed to it. "Platte River," she proclaimed.

Rubin shook his head. "No, my darlin'," he said with a big grin. "A river has water in it." He looked around.

"Don't see no water anywhere, my dear." The Platte was in its seasonal dry spell. It was a shallow river that easily dried up in hot weather, and as easily flooded in heavy rains. Then he stopped and fixed his gaze upon something in the far distance. He kicked his horse into a canter.

They rode until a small Indian village became apparent. It was on the other side of the dry river bed. "I wonder what tribe lives there?" he asked Shadow. He saw a single main lodge type, built with timbers, stone and earth. There were several scattered tipis, too. They slowly rode around the village, not wanting to excite or panic anybody. "That's unusual," he said to Shadow, as he pointed at a small herd of domestic cattle.

They both saw it at the same time. Beyond the Indian village, farther up into the valley, a thin wisp of smoke came from a dwelling's chimney. This was no tipi or lodge; it was a white man's house. They kicked their horses into a full gallop, riding hard, going home to a place they'd never been before.

Startled Indians jumped to their feet as Rubin and Shadow rode through the gate in a cloud of dust. They rode up to the first steppes of the house. Rubin sat upon his horse surveying a troubling sight. Indians were all over the place. He was sure this was his brother and sister in laws house, yet uncertainty directed his thoughts. The Indians looked defiant. Shadow spoke to them in an enquiring tone.

A scream caught everyone's attention. "What the hell is going on in there?" Rubin demanded. Shadow reached for him, trying to calm him as she listened to answers to her questions.

Rubin dismounted and ran up to the closed door. Shadow called to him, "all is well." He wasn't listening as he pushed through the door not knowing the reason for the screams. He was expecting something bad, something wrong.

Rubin tried desperately to evaluate the situation facing him. Rachel crouched in a corner squatting over a pile of bloody clothes. Two other Indian women stood, briskly rubbing what appeared to be a large hunk of raw meat.

Gus stood up from a bench on wobbly legs. There was a ghostly color to his face.

"Gus?" Rubin asked, concerned for his brothers health.

Gus raised a weak hand as if to say hello, then fell forward, flat on his face.

On the other side of the room the Indian mid-wives helped Rachel to her bed, then handed her the baby. It made small soft noises. Rubin saw a little hand reach up. Rachel smiled at her brother in-law.

"Welcome home Rubin! Step over your brother and come see your new nephew."